NEWMAN SPRINGS PUBLISHING
320 Broad Street
Red Bank, NJ 07701

riginally published by Newman Springs Publishing 2020

ISBN 978-1-63692-154-9 (Paperback)
ISBN 978-1-63692-222-5 (Hardcover)
ISBN 978-1-63692-155-6 (Digital)

Printed in the United States of America

FOLLO

First

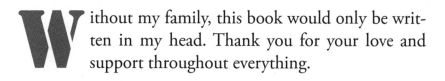ithout my family, this book would only be written in my head. Thank you for your love and support throughout everything.

LAW ENFORCEMENT OATH OF HONOR

On my honor, I will never
betray my badge, my integrity
my character or the public trust.

I will always have the courage to hold
myself and others accountable for our actions.

I will always uphold the constitution,
my community and the agency I serve.

—International Association of Chiefs of Police

FOREWORD

This book was written for entertainment. It was designed to be a coping mechanism for the demons I have battled and are still battling. Many men and women are dealing with issues that have been brought upon them because of the job they were called to do.

We, as law enforcement officers, see people at their worst; we see things the normal person does not and will not. A normal person cannot understand what we see and what we hear; the gurgling last gasp of air from a dying child to the unrecognizable identification of a fatal auto accident to the drug dealer cooking meth in a garage while entertaining their child with video games and a gas mask. To delivering the death notification to parents of a kidnapped and murdered child.

Those images and experiences need to be housed somewhere while knowing that we still get up and do it again and again day after day. There is evil in the world, and it needs to be addressed. The few who will take on that role will be the whipping post of society and will bear that burden.

There are many men and women who have and will have taken the undaunted role as a UC officer. What I did did not reinvent the narcotics operative position; all I did was put my stamp on it. There are many things I did wrong and wish I could have done it differently and better. With that being said, I did do a lot of good things as an officer.

There are two primary things that handcuff police: (1) Lawyers and the politics of deferments and plea agreements, and (2) the politics of the upper echelon and bureaucracy of people in power that don't know or want to know how to combat narcotics.

Narcs have had a bad rap for many years. Uniformed officers look at them as borderline cops. We make our own schedules and wear jeans and T-shirts, grow long hair and beards, and sometimes drink on the job.

But we do put our lives on the line day in and day out. We intermingle with the bad guys without them knowing. We have lunch in the lion's den and supper at Satan's table. The lies and deceitful webs we weave are to save our lives and the ones we love. Our demons sometimes get the better of us and sometimes to the ultimate demise. Our loved ones leave us, our alcohol intake is more than it should be, its restless and sleepless nights, and our comfortable recliner becomes our home. But we do it and we love it, and we would do it again and again.

My position of narcotics operative was the best job I had in law enforcement. It was the most interesting and challenging. It made me think outside the box and utilize resources that I did not know were internally obtainable. Even though laws have changed, the technology has changed, and the politics have changed, there are two constants that will not change—there will be drugs, and there are courageous men and women that will combat it.

Thank you to all the men and women who have put their lives on the line, every day, trying to fight the good fight and battle the evils that walk among us in the shadows. Remember, you are needed, and you are wanted.

Semper Fi.

...And Hell Followed

Written by Phil Queen

CHAPTER 1

When my wife and I headed to the hospital on November 12, it was at that time it became real that I was going to be a father. I had already been a stepdad to Chase for almost two years, but to have your own child is an amazing feeling. The emotions were on full-bore override as I wheeled Tracy through the hospital lobby in the provided wheelchair. The smells in a hospital have always bothered me, maybe that's why I don't like them or maybe every time I'm in a hospital it's for a reason that I don't want to be. But this time was different, my daughter was about to be introduced to the world, and I swore that I would do everything to help and protect her.

What a wonderful day! My beautiful daughter, Samantha, arrived with all her fingers and toes. November 13. She looked so innocent and new, so surreal, my life was now changed, for the better. My wife and daughter were healthy and understandably exhausted. I sat with them in the maternity ward and we were surrounded by fantastic help with the doctors and nurses, an amazing staff. I'd never been a sentimental guy, one that showed emotions or empathy. But that changed now. We would be spending the next couple of days in the hospital before we headed back home. However, Chase and I got a hotel room because there wasn't a place for us to sleep and they wouldn't let me drink beer in the hospital.

My parents came to the hospital to visit as this was their first biological grandchild. They got to hold Samantha, my mom cried and my dad oohed and awed and made baby noises trying to get her to smile. They returned Sam to her mother and we all stepped out to let my wife and daughter rest.

My stepson's 10th birthday was in two days. I found Chase hanging out with grandma and grandpa in the visitor's lobby of the fourth floor. My dad was trying to stomach a cup of hospital coffee that had been brewing for a few hours. I sat down in one of the vinyl and wood hospital chairs and instantly started to doze off. I snapped out of it and tried to regain my bearings. After a short conversation with my parents, I asked Chase what he would like for his birthday, and like a typical ten-year-old, he said he wanted some Hot Wheels.

"Great!" I replied. "Let's go to Walmart and pick out some Hot Wheels and then get lunch. Where do you want to eat?"

Without hesitation, he said. "Subway!"

Chase has been collecting Hot Wheels for a couple of years and has quite an impressive collection for a nine-year-old. Every year for his birthday and Christmas he gets a new series of vehicles and accessories. He collects the cars, trucks, racetracks, service stations, and little towns. He even has a briefcase style container in the shape of a tire and wheel that he carries all the Hot Wheels in.

I returned to the hospital room and asked my wife if she wanted anything while we were out, and she just smiled and said no. She lay in the hospital bed, beautiful as ever, holding onto our new child ever so gently as she slept. I gave her and Samantha a kiss and told them I would see them soon. My daughter looked so beautiful all wrapped up in her blanket that my mother hand made. I just needed one more look before I walked out the door.

Chase and I rode the elevator down from the fourth floor. I usually take the stairs, but Chase, like most children, enjoys riding on the elevator and wanted to push all the buttons. The elevator came to a bouncing stop on the first floor where we were greeted with a ding when the doors opened. A middle-aged White man with a black beard, still wearing his sunglasses, dressed in a long black coat and smelled of Polo by Ralph Lauren, waited for us to exit before he got on. He held the door on his right so we could disembark. I thanked him as we walked by.

Wow, that cologne was powerful. I cannot imagine being stuck on the elevator with him. Chase looked up at me and pinched his nose in disgust, I chuckled and nudged him forward. I'm not sure why but he looked familiar. Why was he wearing his sunglasses? Am I being paranoid? Do I need more sleep? Probably. I turned to get one more glimpse to see if it would jar my memory. He stood in the center of the elevator, alone, grinning as the doors closed. I shook my head in frustration.

We exited the hospital lobby and walked through the chilly Iowa November air toward my Bronco. *I wish I had remote start on this old thing*, I thought to myself. We jogged to the parking spot where the truck waited for us. Chase jumped in and began rummaging for his safety belt. I started the 1995 Ford Bronco XLT and felt the powerful V8 fire up. Chase expressed a sense of satisfaction of the rumble, to be honest, I enjoyed it as well. My Bronco was nicknamed "Not OJ's" due to the fact that it was the same year and color as the one that OJ Simpson had in the infamous car chase in California. I get a lot of comments about it, usually "did you do it?" And "where's the knife?" you know, because I look so much like OJ.

I inserted a CD into the Alpine stereo and cranked up Metallica as we exited the hospital parking lot. We both executed the "rock-on" hand signal and head banging as we drove through the bustling town to Walmart.

A practice that I have picked up since becoming a police officer is to park at the opposite end of the parking lot from the store. Yes, it's a little walk, but it gives me time to assess the area and make sure no one is following me. This is something that I explained to Chase. He thinks it is cool we do this, and he looks around like he knows what he's looking for. I think it's important to explain to Chase different safety practices and someday I will share these safety measures with my daughter. We made our way across the parking lot and entered the store.

Once inside the busy big box store, we scanned the area for the sign that pointed to the toys. Why, I'm not sure, Chase knew exactly where to go and went right to the toy section and located the Hot Wheels. The pre-Black Friday sales had started and apparently, we arrived at Walmart at the busiest time of day. The customers were bustling and scurrying throughout the aisles trying to find the perfect Christmas gifts by the townsfolk at Walmart of course.

Chase began scouring the selection and found a couple that he liked: a police SUV, a fire truck, a yellow Porsche

911 Carrera, and a red Camaro Z28. I jokingly told Chase to put the fire truck back and pick out a cool car.

He looked at me puzzled and said, "Why?"

"I'm just kidding, you can have it." I said as I gave him a little shove. Chase doesn't understand my sarcasm, but most people don't.

While Chase was looking through the toy cars, I noticed two men and a woman walking together past the aisle opening. When I say I noticed, what I mean is, I caught out of the corner of my eye three people walking past the entrance to the aisle. I didn't really think anything of it other than one of the men looked familiar. Does that mean anything? Not really. In crowded places my senses get more heightened and acute.

A White male in his twenties turned his head toward me as he was walking by. And in that quick glance, I recognized him as Brad. Brad was a twenty-five-year-old White guy that jumps from house to house and typically lives on the floor wherever he can. He has not shaved for a week and probably hasn't showered in that same amount of time. His black Carhartt hoodie sweatshirt that he received for Christmas one year was his prize possession, even though the front pouch was ripped, the cuffs were frayed and it was riddled with burn marks from cigarettes and cooking Meth. He was wearing stolen black Nike tennis shoes and faded, dirty blue jeans. His dark brown ratty hair complimented his ensemble as he fit in with the rest of the tweakers in central Iowa.

The three dopers continued walking. Other customers entered and exited the aisle, Chase adjusted his red stocking hat and then his glasses as he perused the other toy cars. He mumbled something to himself as he contemplated his next selection. He was oblivious to anything that has happened, as he should be, he did not know what I knew. I stood a little closer to Chase and told him that we need to wrap this up and go get some lunch. He asked for one more Hot Wheel.

"Yeah, pick one out, quick." I replied as I reached for my beltline to verify my Glock was still there. I knew my Glock was still there, it was just a little reassurance. I struggled for a smile as I watched the pleased, soon to be ten-year-old pick out another much-wanted toy.

I carry my Glock in my waistband without a holster for a couple of different reasons. When I'm on duty, in uniform I carry my sidearm in a holster on my right side. If I'm in a high stress situation my right hand instantly goes to my right side where my gun is. When I'm off duty I carry it in two different positions for two different reasons. I carry it in my right waistband when I'm off duty because I am accustomed to carrying it that way when I'm on duty. When I'm undercover I carry it in the small of my back. I do this because I can get to it with either my left or right hand. Also, carrying a gun in the small of your back and without a holster is not "cop like."

The following is a brief history regarding Brad. I purchased marijuana from Brad about two months ago on three different occasions. My informant, Timmy, and I went to the mobile home park where Brad lived. I didn't know Brad lived there. Hell, I didn't know Brad lived anywhere. I had not thought about him since I arrested him two or three years ago in a small town where I was a uniformed police officer.

When we arrived at the trailer where I was initially going to buy some marijuana or Meth, the targets we had been working for a few weeks were not home. Timmy told me he knew another guy that sold weed a couple trailers away.

It was about eighty-five degrees and ninety-nine percent humidity that day. I was wearing my old dirty jeans and my biker colors that I had designed for undercover work. The vest trapped in the heat and I had a horrible case of swamp ass, but it helped conceal the recording device which I had lining the seam up to the left lapel. Plus, it covered my Glock and honestly, made me look like a badass.

Pale Riders MC was the motorcycle club I invented. This was the only set of colors in existence. The top rocker, "Pale Riders", the bottom rocker, "Iowa" and the center patch was a design that I came up with while drinking beer with a buddy, Nick, while in my garage one night as we worked on a Harley. A circle center patch with a Grim Reaper riding a white horse wielding a big ass hammer jumping through flames. A quote started at the top of the patch and finished on the bottom, "Behold I saw a pale horse, its rider named death, and hell followed." It resembled the artwork of a Molly Hatchet album cover. I will get more in detail about the colors later.

We walked three trailers to the north and Timmy jumped up onto the front porch of the old faded blue mobile home and knocked on the door. I stayed in the vacated white rock parking area in front of the trailer. Timmy stood there swaying back and forth and snapping his fingers and bobbing his head like he was dancing to the song in his head. I watched in amazement that *this jackass just doesn't have a clue*, which is a thought I had go through my head numerous times during my adventures with Timmy. A moment later the door opened and there stood... Brad.

Well, Shit, I thought. *Brad's going to recognize me and make a big deal about me arresting him.*

But he didn't. Timmy introduced me as his cousin from Des Moines and we were looking for some "shit." Brad asked how much, Timmy turned and looked at me.

"How much?" He repeated.

I held up my right index finger to indicate "one".

Timmy looked perplexed and asked, "Ounce?"

"No, pound." I corrected him.

Timmy turned back to Brad and held up his right index finger and repeated, "One pound."

Brad, without saying a word, turned back inside and shut the door. Timmy looked back at me and shrugged his shoulders. I was wearing my sunglasses so Timmy could not see me glaring at him.

I mimicked him with a shrugged shoulders gesture and said, "What the fuck?"

Timmy mouthed the words "I don't know" and began to walk down the steps toward me. The door opened back up, Brad stepped halfway out the door with a brown paper Burger King bag in his right hand and said, "Five hundred."

Timmy stopped and turned back toward Brad and held out his hands as if he was about to receive his diploma. I pulled out my black leather wallet from my right back pocket and opened it, trying not to make eye contact with Brad but still watching his hands and the front door in case somebody stepped out with a shotgun. The chain on the wallet clanked as I counted out five hundred dollars in stuck together 100, 50 and 20 dollar bills.

Brad said to Timmy, "Money first, asshole."

Timmy jumped off the steps and bounded to me with his hand outstretched. I handed him the cash, he turned and jumped back up on the porch. Timmy handed Brad the money and Brad gave him the bag, then slammed the door without saying a word. Timmy tossed me the bag of poor-quality weed from the porch as he jumped off.

"A pound, dude, that's awesome!" he exclaimed, as he tried to high five me.

"Shut up!" I whispered loudly. "Let's get out of here."

We got back to my truck and I called my handler, "You got all that, right?"

"Yes, sir," was the response on the phone.

Since that day, I purchased weed from Brad two more times in accordance with the County Attorney's recommendation for three controlled buys before we arrest him. That is not a law or a rule, but it is good practice. By doing three controlled buys it shows a pattern of distribution. If I were to only buy from Brad one time, his lawyer could show that it was an isolated incident and he only did it once because he was hard up and needed the money. The other two times were just as easy. All three times were video, and audio recorded by my handlers.

After the third purchase, the sheriff's department waited about two weeks, obtained search and arrest warrants and then arrested Brad for distribution of controlled substances.

CHAPTER 2

I didn't recognize the other two people with Brad this November day in Walmart. The White male was about the same age as Brad and the other was a White female in her late thirties or early forties. Judging by their clothing and hygiene, they were in the same line of work as Brad.

The female had faded pink hair in a messy ponytail and a tattoo of three stars on the right side of her neck. They went from small to big on the back side of her neck to below her ear. Her clothes were tattered and ratty and she was wearing a puffy dark gray coat with fingerless cotton gloves, one blue and one red.

The unidentified male was wearing dirty military woodland camouflage pants with a black Harley Davidson t-shirt and white long underwear shirt underneath. He was wearing a sweat stained ball cap backwards with an unrecognizable logo on the front. He had a distinctive walk with a limp favoring his left leg.

I inched to the end of the aisle where I watched them pass and then turned the corner but lost sight of them. I could smell the stale smoke and body odor that they left behind in a vapor trail.

Brad doesn't know I am a cop, but he does think I am the one that narced on him to the cops. I only know this because when he was arrested, he made a comment to another inmate that he was going to deal with me when he got out. That comment made its way back to me through a jailer that knew a police officer that knew me. The Law Enforcement version of the game 'telephone'.

As a police officer, we hear threats from people quite often, at some point, you dismiss it along with all the insults and accusations. However, as a Narc, threats become a little more serious than an idle threat from a random person. Especially if they don't know you're a cop and think you're a just another doper. Drug dealers take it personally when they are arrested and their product and money are seized.

A little more history about Brad: When I was a uniformed officer in the first town I worked in, I arrested him for possession of marijuana and Methamphetamine. Then, when I bought weed from him a few years later he did not recognize me and had no idea who I was. But the circle he runs with all thought I was a DEA Agent because I was the "new" guy and it had to be me that turned them in. Well, it was me, but I am not a DEA Agent.

I went back to where Chase was in the toy aisle as he continued to decide over this car or that truck. He never left my sight, as I was only twenty or so feet from him.

I instructed him. "Take yer cars to the clerk and don't stop an' talk to anyone. When ya get to the clerk tell them to call the police right now 'cause your dad is gonna need some help. Tell the clerk to tell the police that I am a cop and I'm wearin' a dark ball cap, flannel shirt and blue jeans. You got all of that?"

Chase could tell something was wrong by the tone of my voice. I placed my hand on his left shoulder and guided him toward the main aisle. Chase nodded his head in acknowledgement as I walked him to the end of the aisle. I made sure there was no one in the aisle as I nudged him forward. Chase looked up at me with a concerned look, I winked and smiled at him. *I'll buy you all the Hot Wheels you want if I get through this*, I thought to myself. He began jogging towards the front of the store, toys in hand.

While watching Chase jog to the front, I turned around to my right and saw the three dopers walking toward me, in the primary aisle between the sections. Brad peeled off and went down an adjacent aisle. The nameless male and female continued walking toward me, he with a baseball bat in his hand.

I made my way to the center of the toy aisle and put my back up against the shelving and took a deep breath. I scanned from my left to right, waiting. I could feel my heart beating a little quicker, my mouth became dry, and a bead of sweat developed on my forehead as I mentally prepared myself for what was about to come. I wiped my palms on the fabric on my thighs as I breathed in through my nose and exhaled through my mouth.

Situations like this are not something that a normal person endures frequently. When one thinks *What would I do?* We as police don't think *what would I do*, we just do it. We can curl up in the fetal position and hope for the best, or we can react and counteract. This is a true test of wills and how to regulate fear. And I get to test my gumption in aisle ten at Walmart.

I reached down to my right waist band and removed my Glock Model 23, 40 S&W. I grasped the rear of the slide and pulled it back to its full extension at which time

I released it, filling the void of the empty chamber with the silver encased Black Talon that will soon be the leader of the assault. I held the polymer and steel firearm in my right hand and crossed my arms to cover my weapon but kept it pointed in the direction of my-soon-to be target. If these guys left the area and some innocent people entered the aisle, I did not want them to see me standing there with a gun in my hand.

I looked up to check the location of the aerial video recorders and to make sure it could clearly make out my face which would help me in court later. I stood there for what seemed a few minutes but was perhaps less than thirty seconds when at the entrance to the toy aisle from my left appeared Brad.

Brad had a pissed-off look about him, but more importantly he had a gun in his right hand swinging back and forth nervously. I heard something to my right, and it was the other two. Brad looked at them and at me, and I moved my left arm just enough so he could see my Glock. His eyes got big and he took a step back from the aisles' entrance. I then turned to my right and showed the man and woman my right hand. They both took a step back and to the side as if it were a dance move.

I scanned the area, looking left, right, and left. The anticipation was endless. Brad reappeared with the gun pointed in my direction. His finger on the trigger, the hammer cocked, he fired. The cylinder rotated and the muzzle flash was blinding, the report of the gasses exploding from the gun startled me even as I watched the scene unfold. The first round lodged in the shelf to my right, not even close to hitting me. I heard screaming. The echo from the pistol was deafening as I was not expecting it. Auditory exclusion had not set in yet.

I briefly gathered my bearings and fired four rounds not focusing on the sights, just the target. The trigger pull was effortless and cadenced, two sets of double taps. The first striking Brad in the right forearm which was holding the gun. The force threw his arm away from my direction subsequently firing another round from his revolver into the floor at my feet and ricocheting to my right. The next two rounds from my Glock struck him in the chest and right shoulder. The fourth round grazed the right side of his neck as he was falling backward to the ground.

I felt a horrendous blow across my right shoulder and fell to my knees. The unknown male hit me with the Louisville Slugger that he stole from the sporting goods aisle to aid in the assault. I fell to my hands and knees with my Glock pinned under the weight of my right hand, when I felt another strike across my mid back, and then another and another. As I was collapsing, I fell to my right, rolled away, grasped the gun in a proper firing position and pointed my pistol at center mass of the foggy figure holding the long object. I held my breath to alleviate the pain, my mind was mush and my body ached as if a truck hit me.

The reports of my firearm cleared the cobwebs as I lay on my back trying to focus on the body now falling on top of me. Three rounds striking the abdomen and chest cavity of the assailant. The unknown man fell on top of me, dark red blood trickled out of the wounds onto me. With my left hand I shoved the body off me and turned my attention back to Brad, not knowing if he was still in the fight. My head was pounding, the smoke from the gun powder, the ringing in my ears, and the screaming are all symptoms of a chaotic scene indicative of the fog of war.

I'm soaked with blood while lying on the cold tile floor of aisle number ten, fortunately, not my blood. I can feel the blood on my face and in my eyes and mouth. This guy smells so bad, and my hands are sticky from the blood coagulating. His legs are pinning mine from his dead weight, I frantically kick them off me and attempt to roll out and away. The unknown woman vanished in the sea of panicked shoppers and is nowhere to be found.

I hear the faint running footsteps getting louder as they get closer and can feel the vibrations on the tile floor. Two uniformed police officers appear with their weapons trained on me. They are yelling contradicting orders at me telling me to, "drop the gun" and "get on the ground" and "let me see your hands." I am already on the ground, my hands are up, and my Glock is on the ground next to me.

I shout, "I'm a cop, I'm a cop, don't shoot!" I look right at the bigger of the two officers and again yell, "Don't shoot! Don't shoot!"

My ears are ringing due to the blows to my back and/or the shots being fired. I would say both. The bigger officer reached down and took ahold of my gun and told me to turn over, which I did, but not gracefully, so he was kind enough to assist me. Blood is slippery and difficult to gain traction and maneuver on a tile floor.

He put my hands behind my back and proceeded to handcuff me. Now on my stomach, I turned my head to my right and there lay the mystery male staring at me with empty, lifeless eyes. I turned my head back to the left toward the merchandise shelves. The other officer secured Brad's gun and checked his vitals. He looked at his partner and shook his head to say, *he didn't make it.*

The officer that cuffed me called someone on the radio, but I couldn't make out what he was saying. I then heard a response of "10-4" emerge from the static of the handheld radio.

"Can you guys help me up? This is really uncomfortable." I asked the two officers as they secured the scene.

The older officer told me to "sit tight" and to "not move." As he was securing the Louisville Slugger, he slipped and fell in the blood that had accumulated around the unknown tweaker. He regained his composure and checked himself over realizing he now has to throw out a perfectly good uniform.

Keep in mind, this scene is a scene that no matter how much an officer trains for, they really don't know how they will react when or if it happens. The two officers, God bless them, had never been in this situation and for them to react and run to my aid, even though they didn't know what they were doing is commendable. So, I gave them some leniency on not helping me up sooner.

A Deputy Sheriff, whom I recognized, and another police officer, in plain clothes arrived.

Deputy Lee saw me on the floor, "Phil! Holy shit! Get these cuffs off him!" The bigger officer looked at Deputy Lee in confusion.

"Never mind, I'll do it!" Deputy Lee said, as he bent down and inserted the handcuff key into the hole and turned it to free my left hand.

He helped me up and saw that I was covered in blood. I explained to him that it wasn't mine. I was still woozy from the blows to my back and uneasy on my feet. Deputy Lee took me by my right arm and escorted me to the center aisle and removed the other cuff. I leaned on the center aisle product display and tried to catch my breath. Deputy Lee asked me if I knew these guys as he handed me my pistol. I told him I knew Brad and pointed to him.

"The other guy's his buddy. There's a woman with them, did anyone find her?" I asked while putting my finger in my left ear and moving it back and forth trying to clear plugging as if water were in my ear.

Then it dawned on me...

"Chase!" I yelled. "Where's Chase?!"

"Who's Chase?" Deputy Lee asked.

"My son, Chase! He was with me. I sent him to the front of the store to call the cops." I explained as I stood upright to attempt to locate him.

"He must be the one that called then, I'll find him." Deputy Lee said calmly as he put his hand on my shoulder.

He turned away from me and started walking briskly toward the front of the store. I ventured toward the front of the store following Deputy Lee, still covered in blood and foggy headed. I focused and scanned left to right, near to far as I arrived at the checkout area. I spotted Chase by the ATM and made my way to him as people stared at me.

"Chase, you ok?" I asked, he nodded and smiled.

I asked him if he did what I said, and he said yes. I questioned which clerk he talked to and he pointed to an older lady wearing a blue smock behind the counter. I walked up to the counter and showed her my badge and whispered, "thank you."

She struggled with a smile because of the entire incident which just occurred in her store and my unsightly appearance. Chase and I walked out of Walmart and across the parking lot to my Bronco. I put my hand on Chase's shoulder and walked him toward the truck.

When we got back to my truck, I looked at Chase and smiled, "Let's keep this between us and not tell your mother until later."

"Can we still go to Subway?" He asked.

"Damn right we can!" I replied, putting the truck in gear.

CHAPTER 3

When I was in eighth grade growing up in the middle of Iowa, I was playing baseball, football, basketball, attending church, chasing girls, and ditching homework. Everything typical of a fourteen-year-old boy in the Midwest. At that age, the only real information that I had about undercover narcotics work was that of watching *Miami Vice*, *Hill Street Blues*, and other police shows.

Miami Vice really stood out when I was that age. Watching Don Johnson drive around in the Testarossa Ferrari and talking to all the beautiful women of Miami, hanging out with his partner, Tubbs, and having a pet alligator named Elvis. And, of course, busting the kingpins of the dark drug world with hundreds of kilos of cocaine. This is my first impression of being an undercover narcotics officer.

During the career aptitude testing, I recall my high school guidance counselor telling me that I did not have the temperament or the know-how to be a narcotics officer. That really intrigued me that my guidance counselor did not have any idea about me. She just thought that I was living in a dream or had seen too many movies. I think the conversation with the guidance counselor that day sparked something in me more than just watching a 1980s television show with dreadful wardrobes and bad hair but cool cars.

I started my law enforcement career first when I was enlisted in the US Marine Corps. I was stationed in Marine Corps Base Hawaii in Kaneohe Bay in the 1990s. While serving in Third Battalion/Third Marines, Kilo Company Second Platoon, I was "FAPped" to the Headquarters Battalion Military Police. FAP is an acronym for Fleet Assistance Program, which means as a grunt, I was sent to the MPs to help them due to a shortage of marines in the military police unit.

Myself and twenty-five other grunts were sent over to the MPs. This is an interesting concept sending grunts to help MPs when we are typically the ones running from them after a fight at the E-Club. Not that I ever got in fights at the E-Club.

Our typical patrol duty was that of standing at the front gate, the back gate, or at the gate at the entrance pf the flight wing. Our shifts were twelve hours, from 1800 to 0600, was my shift. The other shift being the opposite. Every once in a while, I would get to ride on patrol with one of the "real" MPs. We would conduct traffic stops, respond to criminal complaints, and investigate crimes. After this duty assignment, I definitely made the decision to pursue my career as a civilian police officer.

My first undercover gig also was while in the Marine Corps. A Marine whom I knew was producing and selling fake military identification cards to civilians. Civilians would buy them in order for them to get onto bases and utilize the PX and other military services. This was before 9/11 and prior to Department of Homeland Security, so the ID cards were very generic. Nowadays, they have bar-codes, chips and holograms, and who knows what else.

I assisted NIS (Naval Investigation Services), now NCIS (Naval Criminal Investigation Services), in an under-cover sting. It worked well, and I saw the underside of law enforcement and not just the uniformed aspect. This made me decide that someday I will definitely work narcotics.

Becoming an undercover police officer takes a special kind of person. One must be street smart and be able to uti-lize their wits in a high-stress situation. The Marine Corps assisted with the stress mitigation, but training also helps. First, one must become a law enforcement officer (LEO).

I attended the Iowa Law Enforcement Academy (ILEA) in 2000. I did not receive any training that would help me become a successful undercover officer. Now, I am not saying the ILEA is not a quality academy, quite the opposite really. ILEA is a top-notch academy that has trained thousands of high-quality law enforcement officers for the State of Iowa. ILEA is regarded as one of the best law enforcement academies in the nation. However, at that time, there was not a curriculum for undercover narcotics operations.

Once I graduated from the academy, I went on to my primary duty as a street cop in a small town, I mean really small, like 852 people small. It was located in northwest Iowa and was a typical small town. A gas station, a few churches, a city park, a municipal golf course, a bar, post office, and was surrounded by corn and bean fields. The talk of the town was what sport was going to the state tour-nament or how much rain, snow, wind, lack of rain or heat, which depended on the time of year. But I assure you, the conversations only changed from season to season.

When I moved to this town to be a police officer, it was a culture shock to say the least. I recently moved back to rural Iowa from living in Hawaii for almost four years. I went from the beaches of paradise to the frozen tundra of Iowa. I know some people will argue, but seriously, the beaches of the North Shore of Oahu compared to Main Street on a January Saturday night in Iowa, not really a comparison if you ask me. However, this is where I got my start and the place of my first real drug bust and one of the most high-profile drug busts that I ever made.

One fall Friday night after the local high school football game, our reserve officer, Larry Weston, was riding with me to fulfill his reserve hours' time. At this time, a police reserve officer needed to work at least one shift a month in order to earn the one dollar a month that went into a general fund. The purpose of the reserve officer is to assist the full-time officers with shift work and other various duties. They volunteer their time to gain experience, not money.

On this fall night, we were driving on patrol a little after midnight when we spotted a car driving north on Main Street in the downtown area. When I see a car driving around after midnight and I don't recognize the car, it makes me question why they are in town. A diligent officer recognizes the normal and abnormal on their patrol route.

As I approached the car, the rear lights became brighter, signifying the brakes. The car turned left across the center line and pulled into a diagonal parking spot on the southbound side of the street. As I got closer to the car, I recognized this car to be an early 1990s maroon Ford Thunderbird. This is the same car that I received a BOLO (Be on the LookOut) on earlier in the week to consider the driver to be armed and dangerous and wanted for questioning by the US Marshals in connection to a homicide of a police officer in New Mexico.

"Larry! That's the car that 'Happy' is supposed to be driving!"

"Who the fuck is Happy?" Larry responded, unknowing of the BOLO.

"Happy! Happy! The guy that killed that cop in New Mexico!"

"What the fuck are you talking about, and why the fuck would he be here?" Larry questioned. Larry cusses a lot.

"Okay, so here's what I need you to do. I'm going to pull him over, and I want you to go up to the passenger side with your gun in your hand but don't point it at him. I'm going to go up to his side and keep him there until the State Troopers get here." I instructed him.

I radioed to dispatch with the plate information and that I was conducting a traffic stop at the 300 block of Main Street. I requested backup from any county deputy or Iowa state trooper in the area. I could tell by the fluctuation in the young dispatcher's voice when she responded that she knew I was serious.

"Ten-four, car two. Any additional deputies or troopers in the area of car two at this time? He is requesting immediate back up for 10-99 possible 10-32." Even with the background static, her voice came across the radio sounding stressed.

In police lingo, 10-4 is acknowledgment of the radio traffic, 10-99 means a possible warrant hit or stolen car, and 10-32 signifies a possible firearm present. I heard something garbled on the radio in response but was unable to make out what was said because I was busy exiting my squad car and clearing leather. I was out of the car, which was directly behind the T-Bird in an angled position with my front bumper five feet from the rear bumper of the T-Bird, my emergency red and blue lights activated.

I yelled at the huge man, "Stop! Put your hands on top yer head! Stop moving!"

He continued to walk toward the apartment door between the two businesses. I sidestepped from behind my squad car door and yelled again, with my sidearm pointed at center mass.

"Stop moving! Police! I said stop moving!"

The giant man, and when I say giant, I mean six foot eight inches tall and 325 pounds, with long blonde hair and a gnarly mountain man beard. This was the largest target I've ever pointed my gun at other than maybe a car. He turned toward me ominously, tilted his head down, and raised his left hand to his face to shield his eyes from the blinding lights.

"What the fuck do you want, boy?" His deep, raspy voice echoed between the downtown businesses.

It sounded like Happy had been smoking his entire adult life. He adjusted his stance to be squarer with me as I stood about fifteen feet away by the front of my squad car.

35

Larry inched his way to the front of the T-Bird on the passenger side to utilize the engine block as cover if this goes sideways, good thinking Larry!

Across my radio, I heard an excited male voice. "10-0! 10-0!"

I wasn't sure who it was because I didn't recognize the car number, but I knew what 10-0 meant. Ten-zero is a ten code we used for "use extreme caution." If an officer knows the person another officer is dealing with is dangerous, they will or should call out to the officer "10-0" to get that officer's attention. When the trooper called out "10-0," the hairs on the back of my neck stood up, just like they said in the academy they would. However, I already knew to use "extreme caution" with this fella.

With my weapon still trained on Happy, I instructed him to get on his knees; he did not comply. I told him again, he mumbled something incoherently and slowly lowered himself to his right knee, then the left, all while having his hands interlocked on the top of his head. His long blonde hair swaying in the fall breeze and his steel cold eyes piercing through my soul as if to say, *I'm going to eat your heart.* He didn't actually say that, but he didn't need to because I got the message, "Lima Charlie."

I could feel my hands start to shake because of the adrenaline and brisk air, but I had to hold calm. I do not want this monster to see that I'm frightened or nervous. I do not want him to see any sign of weakness that he could exploit. I could hear the sweet sound of the rhythmic sirens approaching town, feeling that sense of assurance that my brothers are here to watch my back.

I hope these are the biggest, baddest state troopers in the state of Iowa, I thought to myself. We stood in the same position, which seemed like an hour, but actually, was only about two or three minutes.

As the two troopers pulled up behind each other, they exited their squad cars. The first trooper came to my location, and the other went to where Larry was standing. As they approached, they drew their weapons. Neither one pointed them at Happy, they kept them at the position Sul. Trooper one, Erik, asked me if I frisked him yet, I told him no and that I was waiting for him to show up.

I asked Erik if he knew about the BOLO; he responded with a nod and a "yep."

"Let's get him in cuffs," Erik said, still trained on him as if he were a Pointer pheasant hunting.

"On me," I said, not taking my eyes off Happy as I duckwalked to him with my Beretta 96 pointed at his center mass.

Heel to toe, heel to toe, I walked an exaggerated crouched position to Happy and circled around him to his back. Erik had his pistol pointed at Happy now while I "holstered" my sidearm. As soon as I put my gun in the holster, Happy quarter-cocked his head as if something inside said attack now. I reached out and took ahold of his right wrist to bring it to me; he clenched up, not releasing his hands from the top of his head.

"Let go of your hands," I said in a calm authoritative voice. He didn't let go.

I repeated the order. "Let go of your hands."

This time quite a bit more serious, as if there wasn't going to be a third time. He released his grip so that I could bring his right hand to me. I placed a cuff on his wrist and cinched it to the point that I could get my thumb in between his wrist and the cuff. I held on to the vacant cuff and reached up for his left wrist. As soon as I did this, in one fluid motion, he swung his left arm forward and using his weight to throw myself forward toward Erik, with me attached to his wrist.

I unwittingly let go of the handcuff and fell over on top of Happy as he fell forward. I don't think that was his intention, but that's what happened. The whole thing happened in an instant, and while I was on his left side of his back, Happy was reaching through the entanglement, grasping at my duty belt trying to unhook it.

This is a trick that criminals teach each other, when they are in a fight with a police officer, unhook the duty belt and they will protect that instead of fight. This is somewhat true, however, earlier I said that ILEA is one of the best police academies in the nation, and we did a lot of weapon retention drills in defensive tactics class, so I knew how to counter this move.

I rolled over to my right side, the side my holster is on and applied pressure with my body weight, trapping the holstered weapon under me. Erik jumped on and gained control of Happy's left arm. Happy was holding on to my duty belt until I rolled away from his body to my right. This strain forced him to let go, and I was able to regain control of his right arm.

38

By now, the other trooper got in the mix and was able to assist us getting the cuffs on Happy while he was on his stomach, face down on the downtown sidewalk. Larry held his position, taking in the action with a satisfied smirk.

We got him cuffed and gained our composure while we checked each other over for missing equipment and injuries.

"We all good?" Erik asked.

I double-checked myself and gave a thumbs up. *I gotta quit smoking*, I thought to myself.

I motioned for Larry to come to me, trying to catch my breath. I instructed Larry. "Larry, stay 'ere an' watch him. Don't let him get up or sit or move. Got it?"

Larry nodded without taking his eyes off Happy. I went to my squad car and found my bottle of water. I removed the cap, hands still trembling. I took a sip, then another, then a big gulp, and wiped the excess from my mouth. I looked down at my left hand and saw that it was bleeding and shaking. What the hell? I thought. I had a two-inch incision on the outer part of my thumb between my first knuckle and my watch.

I turned and looked at the troopers and Larry and recognized they were fine. I went to my "go bag" in between the two front seats and retrieved a small bandage and a roll of athletic tape to stop the bleeding.

Returning to the other officers, I said, "Let's pat him down before he tries anything stupid again."

After I put my black leather frisk gloves on, which was tricky in itself with that athletic tape and my hands trembling from the adrenaline dump. I searched Happy starting at his head, to his collar, his left arm, right arm, and his waist. At his waist, I found a brown leather pouch with a snap cover on the right side of his belt. Inside was a brown and yellow Buck knife with a three-and-a-half inch locking blade. I removed the knife and handed it to Larry. Happy turned his head toward Larry to see what he was doing with his knife.

I continued the search. In his right front key pocket of his jeans, I found a small clear baggie with light brown powder, presumed to be methamphetamine. I handed that to Larry as well. This is a popular hiding spot that dopers use to stash their personal use. It is overlooked by many officers because it's not seen and primarily forgotten. I will share a horror story about that at a later time.

I searched further and found a much larger clear baggie in his left sock. This was the size of a baseball shoved down the top of his sock, and the top of the sock was rolled over to keep it from falling out.

Once we finished searching Happy, I placed him in the back of my squad car. This was not as easy as one would think simply because he is huge. We got him stuffed in there, so he was sitting with his back against the passenger side rear door, and his feet were on the floor behind the driver's side. With a cage between the front and back seat, there is not a lot of room for a normal size person, let alone a giant, so we had to improvise.

The State Troopers began searching Happy's car, which I joined after we secured him in the backseat. Larry stayed with Happy and made sure he was comfortable. I want to have another satisfied customer by the time I get him to the jail. During the search, we hit the jackpot. The troopers found a black Colt 1911, .45 ACP with a brown wood grip under the driver's seat. The serial numbers had been filed off as well as the front sight.

The front sight being removed proved to be interesting. I have been shooting for about five years at this point and had never heard of such a thing. I presumed you want the front sight for better target acquisition. Happy filed off the front sight so it would not snag on anything when he removed it from the holster. This is a trick that quick draw gun fighters from the Old West would do, and so did Happy. Along with the 1911, we found three full magazines, and a box of 45ACP Black Talon hollow point ammunition in the center counsel.

A duffle bag was found in the trunk that contained numerous items that are consistent with drug trafficking. Some of those items included a baggie full of empty clear baggies; two digital scales; road maps of Iowa, Illinois, Wisconsin, and Minnesota all with lines on specific roadways and circled towns with numbers written in Sharpie next to the towns. Another lock blade Buck knife, multiple lighters, pliers, $5,350 in $100, $50, $20, $10, and $5, and two more boxes of .45-caliber Black Talon ammunition. And last but not least, a ledger with names, addresses, phone numbers, amounts paid, amounts owed, and quantity of product.

Are you kidding me? All this because a guy made an illegal U-turn in front of a police car. Holy shit! I'm going to get officer of the year! I didn't, but that's a different story.

Happy is a long-time member of the Sons of Violence Motorcycle Club (SOVMC) and search warrants were conducted at his residence in the adjoining county. During that search, more evidence was discovered, including more firearms, ammunition, $40,000 in cash, an Uncle Fester Meth cookbook, more scales, and drug paraphernalia. Happy is a felon and subsequently cannot be in possession of firearms or ammunition, which were subsequently two of his numerous charges. After it was all said and done, I contacted a Special Agent with the Alcohol, Tobacco, and Firearms (ATF), which they gladly took off my hands. They also contacted agents with the Drug Enforcement Administration (DEA) and continued the investigation.

At this point, I no longer had any involvement with the case. All I know is, there were more arrests made in multiple states. I did, however, testify in Federal Court in Sioux City, Iowa, twice regarding the initial arrest of Happy. When Happy appeared in court with his attornies, he had a nice haircut and trimmed goatee. If it were not for his huge stature, I would not have recognized him.

Happy was convicted and mandated to serve sixteen years in Club Fed.

CHAPTER 4

When people hear about the state of Iowa, they primarily think corn and wrestling. Both are true; however, Iowa has a lot to offer and is a very interesting state. In a state of two and half million people, there are more livestock than humans. The winters are extremely cold and the summers sweltering hot. We enjoy all four seasons, sometimes all in one week. Iowa has three division one colleges, numerous lakes, golf courses, and state parks; the people are friendly and caring and many, many hard working, God-fearing people. Another thing we have that is not a bright point is meth labs.

In 2003 and 2004, Iowa Law Enforcement located 2496 meth labs. That's 3.4 meth labs per day in two years. New laws were established for purchasing pseudoephedrine and anhydrous because of the meth cooks. Task forces were formed, and undercover operations were abundant. The first DEA Basic Narcotics school was formed in Iowa through the MCTC (Midwest Counterdrug Training Center) in 2003, which I attended.

The instruction provided proved to be second to none and more than helpful and useful with the investigations, which I conducted thereafter. Prior to this school, I was winging it. It was such a good school; I went again nine years later for a refresher. All of this would aid in the investigations and convictions of meth manufacturers to ensure the safety of the Iowa people.

PHIL QUEEN

As a police officer, I would assist in the war on meth and be instrumental in some key investigations that helped take many pounds, thousands of dollars, a few guns, and numerous drug dealers off the street. In twenty years as a police officer, I am responsible for over fifteen hundred arrests. One third of which were drug and gun-related.

To put that into perspective, there are more people in the city of Chicago than in the state of Iowa. As a lowly undercover narcotic operative, my job proved to be quite difficult. The bigger cities and metropolitan locations produce large quantities of drugs and money and usually what the movies and TV portray. But I assure you, the drug issues we have in Iowa are real and a significant problem. The two interstates that run through Iowa are I-35 and I-80 and are the pipelines for drug, gun, and human trafficking for the United States.

I conducted numerous undercover narcotic operations in a span of about three years. This next particular operation was not a long one, but it did do a lot of damage in the drug world of central Iowa. I learned a lot on this operation, especially things not to do. Undercover work is done by trial and error and is extremely unpredictable.

Deputy Pete Thompson and I met each other a few years ago on a multi-jurisdictional operation. He was a deputy sheriff with a small county in Iowa and a K-9 handler and actually very good K-9 handler whose known all over the United States as a K-9 trainer. Pete had been a deputy for probably about twelve years at that time.

Pete called me up one day and told me that he was working a case on a couple of guys that were selling meth

44

in a local bar in his county. I agreed to meet with him at a predetermined location so we can go over all the specifics on the individuals that he was investigating. This would have been in the early 2000s when Pete and I started working together as undercover officers.

The technology back in the early 2000s was not that of today and was a little bit more difficult. We did not have the social media or some of the other technology that we would use in 2020. I used a recorder that resembled a key fob for a Chevy vehicle. I would push the unlock button, and it would record. I would push the lock button, and it would stop recording. Then to download the recording, I would plug in the USB to a computer. At that time, it was high speed.

Pete and I met in the middle of the afternoon at a remote park his county. I hopped in the front passenger seat of the truck; he was driving a black Ford F150 crew cab pickup. We exchanged pleasantries and made off-the-cuff jokes. Pete then got down to business and opened a manila file folder. In the file were numerous photographs, quite a few documents regarding the suspects or targets that he wanted me to work. One of the main guys goes by the name of Glenn. He was big into helping meth dealers find pseudoephedrine and anhydrous. He is what we would call a "smurf."

Now, Glenn was not the most intelligent fella. He dropped out of high school his junior year and worked odd jobs including construction and a handyman. Glenn was a White male, about five foot nine inches, thin build, and in his early thirties. He was single for the most part, and his family lived on the other side of the state. Glenn was living in a trailer in a very small town on the edge of the county. He had scruffy brown hair, a five o'clock shadow, and most of his clothes were raggedy and unkempt.

There was nothing specific about his trailer other than his trailer was a normal trailer in middle Iowa. Pete had the meeting set up so we would be going to meet Glenn that night. The initial plan was to do an introduction of me with Glenn in order to get to the primary meth cook.

At 2100 hours: Pete and I went to the Kickstand Bar and sat at a roundtable in the back of the bar where we could watch the front and back door. And still keep the wall to our backs. The Kickstand Bar had been the town's main bar for about sixty years but has changed owners and names several times. It had the typical dark wood bar with scratched countertop and a brass foot rail with backless black bar stools surrounding it. Judging by the cracks and discoloration, they are probably the original bar stools.

This was in a time when the bar patrons could smoke in a bar. Nowadays, you have to go outside to a specialized area the bar designates as the smoking area. The bar reeked of stale beer, cigarette smoke, and that musty smell of mold ingrained in the twenty-five-year-old carpet. Ahhh, home sweet home. I have spent many hours in this type of bar throughout my life; this is the same bar, just a different location with a different name.

There were about fifteen people in the Kickstand this night. A fifties something couple dancing in the corner to "The Whipping Post" by the Allman Brothers. They were dancing like they did in the 1970s reminiscing the Allman

Brothers' concert. Two long hair bikers were playing pool and sneaking glances at the woman dancing. One was particularly interested as if she was an ex-girlfriend.

The bartender/owner seemed like a nice guy, probably in his fifties and clearly a biker. A large "Support Your Local SOV Chapter" sticker was on the right side of the huge bar mirror. I will get into the SOVMC later, but for now it stands for Sons of Violence Motorcycle Club. Bad dudes if you know what I mean.

Pete had this undercover getup he liked to use. He wore a long black hair wig and had these round John Lennon style glasses with rose lenses. His cover story was that he was a construction worker looking for work. He did not look like any construction worker whom I have ever seen, but he knew what he was talking about when it comes to dope and construction work.

I don't know shit about construction and have never done construction in my entire life, so this is a little bit more difficult for me. However, what I did know was Harley-Davidson motorcycles. I have worked on Harleys, ridden Harleys, and hung around some unsavory types that rode Harleys. Pete didn't know anything about Harleys, so it was a little bit more difficult for him to discuss.

We sat at the roundtable sipping on a bottle of Budweiser beer trying to figure out when or if Glenn was going to show up. The red round candle provided a particular ambiance and seconded as a cigarette lighter as we sat at that table for an hour or so. The door opened to our right and in walked Glenn.

Glenn strolled up to the bar and waved to a few people, then ordered himself a drink; by the color of the light brown liquid, it appeared to be whiskey. We sat there for a little bit watching and waiting to see if he would come up talk to us. After about ten minutes, I walked up to the bar and ordered a couple more beers. I asked him how he was doing. Glenn looked at me and shrugged me off.

I put my hand out to shake and said, "Hey, I'm Preacher."

He glared at me and said, "That's supposed to interest me why?"

I reached into my inside vest pocket and retrieved a pack of Marlboro red cigarettes. I set down the pack on the bar after I got a cigarette out. I lit up a smoke. He glanced at me and then looked down to my pack of cigarettes. I keep a pack of Zig-Zag rolling papers in the cellophane wrap of the cigarettes to indicate that I smoke weed. Why else would I keep Zig-Zags in a filtered pack of smokes?

I smiled and said, "Can ya' hook me up?"

"Man, I don't know you. Go away."

I smiled, grabbed my two beers, and walked back over to the table where Pete was sitting.

Pete looked at me and said, "What the hell, dude?"

I sat down in my chair, handed him his beer, and told Pete to give it a couple minutes he will be over. We sat there for probably fifteen more minutes or so talking about nothing, trying to watch everybody coming in and out of the bar. Patrons milled around, attempting to have a conversation over the music, shooting pool, throwing darts, just trying to keep everything cool. A short time later, Glenn walked over to us and sat down without saying a word. We both looked at him, then looked at each other. I looked down at my beer and asked him if I could help him.

Glenn said to me, "I see you smoke."

I nodded as I took a pull of Budweiser.

Glenn confirmed that I was looking for a hook up.

I nodded.

He asked where we were from.

"Sioux City."

He continued the ask and answer session.

"What are you guys doing here?"

"We're meetin' a guy about a Harley, a '65 Panhead to be exact." I continued with my BS story. "His name is Larry somethin' or other."

I could see the wheels turning in Glenn's head, trying to think of somebody named Larry who had a 1965 Harley Davidson Panhead. We discussed Harleys for a little bit. Glenn informed me he has a late nineties' 1200 Sportster. It was not much, but he liked it. He asked us if we had been to "this bike rally or this bike show or that bike show." I informed him that we had. We talked about the topless women, the drag races, the fancy bikes, the drugs and alcohol, and so on and so forth. The conversation shifted and asked him if he could "hook us up" since we are going to be sleeping in the truck tonight.

"Hell yeah," he said excitedly. "I can hook you up, follow me to my house."

We knew were Glenn lived but had never been in his house. It was a mobile home, so the layout was pretty much the same as any other trailer. Glenn lived down the street from the bar. We left the pickup in front of the bar and took a midnight stroll to Glenn's trailer. I thought it would be a good idea to grab a beer for the road. As undercover officers, it is a good idea to fraction a law or two when on the job. The targets seem less suspicious when they see the "UCs" do this.

We arrived at Glenn's humble abode. The trailer sat on an empty lot in a residential neighborhood. It was the only trailer among the single and double-story homes. I'm sure the neighbors loved that he brought down their home values. In small town rural Iowa, there are not many rules with the homeowner's organization.

There was no driveway, so Glenn's maroon 1993 Ford Mustang sat perpendicular with the mobile home in the front yard. His Harley was next to it with the kickstand on a wood block so it wouldn't sink in the soft ground.

Glenn unlocked the door and invited us inside. A dimly lit TV was the security system, making it appear someone was home. The odor of cigarette smoke, body odor, and something rotten in the refrigerator filled the air as we entered the dwelling. The vinyl flooring creaked and shifted as we moved across the floor. Glenn pointed to the brown recliner on the right side of the room, gesturing for one of us to have a seat.

We knew no other people lived there because of prior intelligence. But occasionally, these guys will have some strays stay with them, which were not in the initial intel report. Glenn flipped a light switch; however, there were no overhead lights, but two lamps came on, one next to the couch and one next to the gold faded microfiber recliner.

Glenn sat on the middle of the couch. An old wood coffee table with scratches and names engraved on the top, filled the room between the couch and the television. Playboys, empty and not empty Pepsi, Mt. Dew, and Bud Light bottles and scratch off tickets riddled the table. Glenn reached underneath the table and pulled out a tin that was about six inches wide by eight inches long and three inches deep.

The tin had an oriental dragon design on the lid, which he had trouble removing. Glenn eventually opened the tin and inside contained a collection of Zig-Zag rolling papers and a dime bag of marijuana or maybe a little more.

He got one of the rolling papers out, opened the baggie of marijuana, and sprinkled a little weed in the crease. He rolled it up and with the finishing touch of licking the edge. Glenn inspected the joint with satisfaction and spit the residual taste out of his mouth.

"Hey, you guys want some music on? Check this shit out!"

He grabbed a remote from under the table and pushed some buttons. The music came on instantly at level ten. He turned it down a couple notches because of the displeased look on my face. Zakk Wylde's guitar riffs and familiar voice echoed throughout the mobile home. Great, the cops are gonna get called.

I reached inside the left side of my leather vest that I always wore when I did undercover operations. I had made some secret pockets on the inside where I could conceal items like an extra magazine for my Glock, a listening device, handcuff key, and a fixed blade palm knife.

A palm knife does not look like a traditional knife with a blade and handle. The blade is double-edged and spear-head-shaped, only three inches in length and the handle is a "T" handle that fits in the palm of your hand, hence the name "palm knife." I heard a story about an undercover cop who was handcuffed by some dopers and then beaten. Ever since then, I carry an extra key and knife.

Inside my pocket, I keep a different pack of cigarettes, a pack of Marlboro Lights. I use the Marlboro reds and the Marlboro Lights differently so I could keep them apart. Inside the Marlboro Light box were two already rolled marijuana joints. These joints are not normal marijuana joints; they are fake weed. There was a company from Florida that made a synthetic marijuana to be used by narcs. When burnt, it smelled like weed and when smoked, it felt like you were smoking weed but without the high. It was essentially synthetic weed without THC. It was very convincing.

I retrieved a joint from the pack and lit it on the first strike with my Bic lighter. Zippo lighters are generally not used when smoking weed because of the oil taste that it provides.

"I thought you didn't have any?" Glenn asked inquisitively.

"This is my last one. We'd like to get some more for the road and for the rest of the night."

"Okay, cool."

I took a long drag off my joint and held in for a little bit and then gradually blew it out like I knew what I was doing. I did this a couple more times, and Glenn watched me. Pete was sitting on a vintage gold-colored vinyl and metal kitchen chair that he brought into the living room and placed it strategically facing the front door while still able to watch us. Pete did this in the event if someone came in unannounced, he could react accordingly. He had a better view of the door than I.

I reached my hand out holding the joint between my finger and thumb and gestured to Glenn.

"Here, take a hit off of this shit."

He reached out for the joint, examined it, and blew on the lit end to make the ember glow. Glenn placed the joint between his lips and closed his eyes in satisfaction. He inhaled a nice long drag off it and instantly started coughing. I started laughing, knowing that the stuff was strong. He asked where I got this stuff.

"From a Mexican fella over in Sioux City."

He told me that the stuff he has is not nearly as good as this stuff and asked if I could get some for him.

"I'll see what I can do, but I don't know how soon I'll be back this way. Take a couple more hits and tell me what you think," I said nonchalantly.

Same outcome, he began to cough big deep coughs, but the smile on his face was enormous.

He looked up at me with teary eyes and smiled.

"This is some good shit."

Glenn handed me back my joint, and I took a couple more hits off it. I scraped off the cherry of the joint in the metal Playboy bunny ashtray on the coffee table, then put it back in my cigarette pack. I glanced over at Pete; he was shaking his head with a smirk on his face as to say, *What a dumbass.*

Glenn told me he would sell me the rest of his weed for forty bucks.

I bartered, "Forty? I'll pay thirty."

He thought about it for a second while stroking his scraggly beard, then said, "Fine, I'll take it."

He tossed me what was left of the dime bag. I pulled out my wallet that was hooked onto a chain on the right side of my back jeans pocket. I retrieved a twenty-dollar bill and a ten-dollar bill and handed it to him. Now we have Glenn on felony distribution charges, and he has no idea.

We sat there for another five or ten minutes in the marijuana and cigarette smoke-filled room. I could tell Pete was starting to get annoyed now. He was becoming fidgety and continuously looking at his watch. This is a sign that we need to be elsewhere, but we don't and dopers that are trying to host can get offended and we could lose a later deal. I need to make good friends with Glenn so we can continue this charade, then I get to meet his supplier.

Pete had done some undercover operations but nothing this extensive, usually it was in and out and done. This is going to be one of those operations where it was going to take a lot of time and take a lot of effort and potentially be more dangerous than usual. Pete told Glenn that we need to get going, and head to the roadside park and crash for the night. He reminded Glenn that we are going see that guy about his Harley tomorrow.

We walked out of Glenn's trailer and down the sidewalk toward the bar as he watched us disappear into the darkness of rural Iowa. The streetlights apparently do not work on this street. This is by design. Glenn disabled the two nearest streetlights, so it is more difficult for curious onlookers and intrusive law enforcement to watch his place. It also makes it easier for Glenn to see if anyone is in the area.

As we walked back to our pickup, I glanced over my shoulder to make sure no one was following us. It would be pretty difficult to explain how two veteran cops got jumped by a tweaker.

As we left town, we made a quick pass by Glenn's trailer, a single light was on and then turned off as we drove by. We drove to the sheriff's office and pulled into the garage. The truck's engine stopped and made some final sounds that echoed in the garage. I collected all the evidence from the back seat and walked up to the second floor where Pete had his office. We both reek of stale smoke, both cigarettes and weed and a little bit of beer, too.

Pete's office was in the new section of the remodeled courthouse. Each deputy has their own office with their own phone and laptop. This way, they can talk in private and feel more secure in the building. No one outside of their department is allowed in the offices. Each time I go there, I have to be escorted through the building. It seems like a no-brainer, but my office is like Grand Central Station and completely unsecured. Every city employee has a key to my office.

The sheriff's department has a state-of-the-art keypad with a unique key code to each deputy. They also have their own evidence lockers, which is a nice feature, but there are no checks and balances when it comes to evidence. However, the chain of custody stays uncompromised this way, which is its intention. I entered in all the information and evidence while sitting at Pete's fancy desk with the laptop Pete gave me to type my report. Once my report was done, I handed the laptop to Pete to review the report. This is the boring part of my job and is the part that television and movies fail to show, but who the hell wants to watch a cop movie about writing reports?

I raised my arms above my head to stretch and tried to stifle a yawn. I took a swig of my bottled water, looked at my watch, and told Pete I was going to head for home, and I would talk to him soon.

CHAPTER 5

Two days later, Pete called me and asked if I would be available to come back up and meet with him.

"I'll be up in two hours."

When I arrived, I met with Pete at the county roadside park about twenty-five miles from town. Pete was still driving the same black 2000 Ford F150 pickup. We discussed the operation and how it was going. Pete did not have any new information regarding Glenn other than he heard Glenn received an unknown amount of meth and weed.

Pete obtained this information from a snitch he has working for him. Apparently, she has been his snitch for over two years and frequents the local bars; people trust her with a lot of information. I have never met her and don't know her name, but Pete trusts her.

We agreed this time. Instead of going to the bar to meet with Glenn, we are just going to go to his trailer. Glenn did not have a job, so more than likely, he was going to be home. However, unannounced visits usually meant other people could be at his house. That was a risk we were willing to make.

Pete's snitch later advised him that Glenn has approximately one pound of meth that he received from his source within the last twenty-four hours. This unknown supplier is supposedly a big meth cooker that lives in the country. We don't know him and don't know exactly where he lives. He goes by the name "Zombie." This could be a big deal for us to meet with Zombie.

While going over the specifics with Pete, I double-checked my Glock to make sure I had a round chambered. I patted myself down to make sure my extra magazine was in its pocket in my vest. Then felt for my palm knife handle, good to go. Pete checked the audio and video equipment installed in his pickup while I checked over the money and made sure my backup pistol and AR rifle were in their secured locations behind the back seat.

I also deployed a desert tan MOLLE (Modular Lightweight Load-carrying Equipment) "go bag" with extra magazines, flashlight, batteries, a small first aid kit with a tourniquet and binoculars. We hid all the items behind the back seat in a hunting storage bin. Since I knew I was going to be meeting Glenn, I brought a couple of my "special" joints to trade with him.

"You ready for this, brother," I asked Pete in my gravelly voice as I extended my right hand to him.

"Hell ya, let's do this," he responded, as he grasped my hand with his big mitt.

We jumped in the truck and sped off down the highway to meet with Glenn.

As were cruising to Glenn's town, Pete cranks the stereo up with some pop country from the local country radio station. "My Maria," by Brooks & Dunn was playing as if on cue. I sang along in the best southern falsetto I could muster. I love that song! I never took Pete as a country music fan, but he apparently is.

I pointed to Glenn's trailer as if Pete didn't know where we were going.

He turned to me with a puzzled look and said, "Really? Like I didn't know where we're going?"

I smiled and continued to scan the area. As we arrived, I noticed an unfamiliar vehicle in the yard. A blue Dodge Stratus with Iowa license plates. The front windows were rolled down, and it was parked next to Glenn's Mustang facing the opposite direction.

"Know the car?"

"Nope."

Fantastic, I thought.

Pete drove past the trailer and circled around the block. When we returned, he drove onto the lawn and parked in front of the Dodge and behind the Mustang. I reached down under the center counsel and flipped the switch for the recording devices. Pete and I were both wearing a mic, and the one in the truck is backup. All three are on the same system so we can download them together at the end of the operation. It is a slick and expensive system that Pete's department got with grant money from the Department of Homeland Security.

During this time frame after 9/11, when DHS was formed, there was government money being handed out like candy to kids at Halloween. We were able to get a lot of cool shit that wasn't available before. All we had to do was show it was for the war on drugs. Drugs support terrorism, so it was easy to show the government what we needed to combat the war on terror. I did not get any for my department because of the size, but a lot of other departments and task forces were able to utilize the funds.

I jumped out of the truck and walked up to the front door. It opened before I could get my hand up to knock. This startled me and in turn, startled Pete.

"Jesus, fuckin' Christ!" I stammered as I reached for my gun in my waistband.

"What's up, fellas?" Glenn yelled happily and clearly high. "What are you fucker's doin' here?"

"On our way through so we thought we'd stop in smoke a bowl," I responded as I repositioned my pistol nonchalantly.

Glenn has no idea how close he came to getting ventilated. Now I have to change my shorts.

"Come on in! I gots a surprise for ya fuckers!" Glenn waved us in with his right hand as he steadied himself against the door jamb with his left.

I glanced at Pete and grinned.

"This is going to be good," I mumbled.

He grunted in return.

"Fellas, have a seat." Glenn opened his arms in the direction of the couch. He paused and turned to me, "Did you bring it? Tha good shit, did you bring it?"

"Yep, I got it."

Glenn jumped up and down like a kid on Christmas morning, finding out that he got a new red bike. The whole trailer shook and creaked as he jumped.

Glenn pointed at the guy sitting on the couch and introduced him as Jeremy, then pointed at the girl sitting in the chair, Sarah. Jeremy was the typical middle Iowa twenty-something White guy who works odd jobs to help fuel his addictions of meth, alcohol, and cigarettes.

He sat on the couch chain-smoking generic menthol cigarettes. His brown hair shaved on the sides and back and about one inch on top like a garage Marine high and tight. Jeremy clearly shops at the same tweaker clothing store as Glenn, with the tattered jeans, UFC T-shirt, and beat-up Nike tennis shoes. One added piece to the ensemble was the black grip to a semiautomatic pistol sticking out of his waistband.

Sarah, on the other hand, looked like she just stepped out of a *J. Crew* magazine with her oversized, pink, hooded sweatshirt; tan and tight Capri pants; white loafer shoes; and hair put up nicely in a high ponytail. She sat on the chair drinking out of a wine cooler bottle while smoking a Marlboro Light 100.

Glenn's trailer smelled the same as before but now added an evergreen scented candle to the array of aromas. The candle was giving me a headache. I'm sure it had nothing to do with the strong odor of burnt marijuana.

"Let me get a hit of the good shit." Glenn requested as he put his tatted right arm around my shoulder and gave an uncomfortable squeeze.

I obliged Glenn by reaching into my vest and retrieving the "special" pack of Marlboro Lights. I opened the pack and picked out a pre-rolled joint. I inserted it into my mouth and lit it with my red Bic lighter, inhale, slow exhale. Glenn leaned in, waved the smoke to his face with his palm, and inhaled. His satisfied smile said it all.

"Let me get a hit, bro." Glenn begged.

I handed Glenn the "J." He hastily took a hit, long hit. Then exhaled.

"Dude, come get some of this!" He turned and extended his hand to Jeremy.

Jeremy stood up awkwardly from the couch and stepped to Glenn. Jeremy took the joint and placed it between his lips. He took a long deep draw in and held it. When he blew it out, he doubled over coughing. We all laughed and pointed at Jeremy, including Sarah.

"Look, brother. We're heading to a rally, and I need some white. Hook me up?" I asked Glenn.

"Ya, how much ya need?"

"Ounce."

Glenn's smile shifted to a scowl. He looked at Pete, then to Jeremy, then back to me. He sat on the couch and adjusted his crotch.

"One ounce?" he asked.

I nodded and looked at Pete.

"Ya, I can do that."

I released a suppressed sigh and smiled.

"Awesome!" I answered.

Glenn exited the living room and went into the back room, presumably his bedroom. Jeremy continued to stare at me.

"I know you," he said in a whisper like he was telling me a secret.

"You don't know me, bro," I responded with a gruff authoritative voice.

"You a cop?" Jeremy asked in a smartass accent.

"Yep, I'm a cop and as soon as I buy this shit, I'm going to bust every one of you motherfuckers," I responded with a cop like stance and posture, then busted out laughing.

"You should see the look on your faces!" I pointed at both Jeremy and Sarah as they look perplexed at each other. I took another hit off my joint and placed my right foot on the coffee table, then rested my arms on my bent knee.

I leaned toward Jeremy and asked, "Do I look like a fuckin' cop? Do I look like a pig? Well?"

"Naw, man, you don't. Sorry, brah, gotta ask," he said quietly, looking down to his belt.

Glenn returned and handed me a brown paper bag that was rolled tight around a clear baggie of white powdery substance. I weighed it with my internal scale by bouncing it in my hand.

"Feels right." I confirmed.

"One grand." Glenn requested.

"No problem, brother."

I retrieved my wallet and took out one thousand dollars in hundred-dollar bills, then handed it to him and counted it out, clearly. I did this so the recording devices could pick up my voice so there would not be a question when it came time for court.

"I need you to do something for me." Glenn requested.

His voice sounded more sober and serious than it did three minutes ago.

"Name it, bro."

"I need you to get me one thousand pseudo pills. Think you can handle that?"

"What you need that for? Yer not a cook."

"Don't worry about it. Can you get 'em or not?"

"I'll see what I can do. When you need them by?"

"Sooner the better."

"Gimmee a time frame so I know what I'm workin' with."

"Saturday," Glenn said matter-of-factly.

This time frame gives me an idea of when the cook is going to be cooking another batch. If he needs one thousand pills from me, that means he is probably getting more pills from other people as well. This is going to be a large batch of meth.

"That's a short time to get that much," I said, acting like it was going to be really tough to do.

"If you can't handle it, I'll get someone else," Glenn responded.

"No, no, no, I can get it for you. I'll meet you here Saturday afternoon," I said, reassuring.

"Good, see you then," Glenn said as he walked us to the front door.

We have two controlled buys on Glenn, as well as conspiracy charges once we deliver the pills. This is working better than I thought.

That was not the last time I see Jeremy and Sarah.

CHAPTER 6

On Saturday at about 1600 hours, I arrived at Pete's office. He wasn't there yet so I sat in my truck and waited in the sheriff's office parking lot. Back then, there were no smart phones, so I had to make do with a baseball magazine that I kept in my truck for moments like this. A short time later, Pete arrived in the UC truck.

"What's up, brother?" I asked energetically.

"Not a thing, bro, other than my wife not happy with me since it's our anniversary and all."

"Oh shit, dude, you wanna call it off?"

"Hell naw! I told her we'd celebrate when I get home."

"Cool."

When we got upstairs to the sheriff's department, the sheriff and chief deputy were waiting for us to debrief them on the operation and what the plans are tonight. Since we need a thousand pseudoephedrine pills out of the blister packs, we needed the Chief Deputy to get them out of the evidence room.

We also got a thousand dollars for flash money in case we need it. I had to hand count each and every pill while Pete documented all the cash. He photocopied each bill and logged in each serial number on a currency document form. This is in the event we do a buy/bust, we can confirm the money is in the hands of the bad guys. We don't plan on doing a buy/bust, but sometimes it happens. When you don't take Murphy's Law into account, it will bite you in the ass.

"One thousand pills, exactly. Jesus, that sucked!" I exclaimed, exhausted and rubbing my temples to alleviate a headache.

"Take pictures." Pete ordered as he divvied up the money so we both had some.

"I already did that, boss." I held up the digital camera to show proof.

We sat with the Sheriff, Chief Deputy, two Deputies, two local police officers as well as the County Attorney, who arrived late, of course. I had met one of the deputies prior to today but did not know the other one or either police officer. Both of the officers looked as if they had over five years of experience. I handed out a document packet with all the bad guys' information including photos, locations, vehicles, grid coordinates, our contact numbers, and all the safe words and equipment details.

We explained how everything will go down, where we will be meeting, which people will be with us, what the color of the day is, what the bust signal is, what the aid sign is, what weapons we have, and all communications and channels. The color of the day is red and is the color that identifies us as the officers for all cover officers. The bust signal is, "It's too hot in here for that," and the aid sign is "Superman."

These are very important to know and understand. We went over all the photos and descriptions of the players that will allegedly be at the meet, although we do not know the identification of "Zombie." We even included photos of our smiling faces with the words "Do not shoot this guy" written in red Sharpie.

Typically, as an undercover operative, I do not allow officers who are not in the briefing to be part of the operation. However, there were two deputies who will be joining up with us later because they were on a different assignment during the time of the brief. Pete knows them and can vouch for them.

I was dressed in my familiar biker garb with my beat-up boots, Levi's, a black Harley sleeveless T-shirt, you know, to show off the guns and tats. And, of course, my Pale Riders MC colors. I normally don't wear a bandanna, but for this op, I wore a red one on my head like a thick headband.

Pete was wearing his famous black long hair wig. It looks like a Goth-style hairdo, long straight jet-black hair. He obtained it from a Hollywood movie costume company. He was wearing a black Hurley hooded sweatshirt and woodland camouflage BDU (Battle Dress Uniform) pants with black Adidas tennis shoes. Pete always added a little more flare to his getup—this night, he painted his fingernails black. It looked stupid but funny.

We both kept our badges around our neck under our shirts. Pete had his on a metal chain, and I had a piece of 550 cord tied to a black badge holder. The cord is very strong so my badge can't get ripped off. On the flip side to that, it could be used against me to choke me. I didn't think that through very well. I generally don't have a badge on, but something told me that I needed to have it on tonight.

Pete also wore a bulletproof vest under his sweatshirt. I have only worn a vest on a UC operation one time. I wore it over my T-shirt to a meet with a meth dealer as a sign of distrust of that dealer. I have one in the truck with my other gear, but I won't be wearing it this night.

At 1900 hours: Pete and I left the Sheriff's Office and drove to Glenn's trailer to pick him up. On the way there, I went over all the cameras and mics and conducted sound checks with our cover officers. Pete took a shot of whiskey from a silver metal flask he had lodged between the seats. He handed it to me. I held up my left palm to indicate "no thanks."

I double-checked my Glock 23 to make sure a round was chambered. There was a horror story about a soon-to-be an ex-wife of an officer who took the chambered round out of her husband's sidearm and then inserted the gun back into its holster. He had to shoot a perp that night and when he pulled the trigger, it went "click." The officer/husband was shot and killed by the perp. Ever since I heard that story, I check, double-check, and recheck my weapon. I don't know if it's a true story or not, but it is really messed up, and I always remember to check my pistol.

As we got closer, I closed my eyes. Cleared my head. I inserted myself into the right mind-set. Inside my head, I transformed from a cop to a dirt bag biker who doesn't give a shit about anyone or anything.

Here we go!

As we pulled up to Glenn's trailer, we could see him sitting on the front steps smoking a cigarette. He stood up in anticipation and jogged to the street for us to pick him up. Glenn was holding up his pants with one hand as he rushed to the truck. Pete brought the truck to a stop in a spot so that Glenn would have to run in front of the lights. I opened the door and jumped out.

"Hey, bro! Here, sit in the front seat so you can tell him where to go," I said as I extended my right hand to shake Glenn's hand.

"Great to see you, guys!" Glenn smiled and jumped in the truck.

I sat in the back seat behind Glenn. This was by design. If Glenn decides to rip us off, I have my Glock pointed at him through the back seat. The rounds will tear through the fabric like it is not there. You cannot trust these guys. As we drove down the county blacktop, we joked and called each other names and belched and farted. Glenn was more nervous than usual. Maybe because we were walking in into an ambush or maybe because he is high or maybe he does not like working with Zombie. I lit up a fake joint and handed it to him.

"Oh, that'll work, bro!" He reached out for it without missing a beat.

Now the truck reeks of weed, fake weed mind you.

After about twenty-five miles, Glenn started to watch the area more intently. He had his right hand on the dash while holding a lit cigarette in his left hand, leaning across the center counsel invading Pete's personal space.

"Dude! Quit blowing smoke at me, get over on yer side," Pete irritatingly said.

"Take a left up here at the next gravel road," Glenn said as he ignored Pete's orders and pointed to the left of the truck in the area of a cornfield.

Pete knows this area and knows that the west side of the county road is a different county. Criminals do not care or take into consideration jurisdictional lines. Law enforcement does. Our cover officers were following us at a safe distance but will soon see us turn left into the next county. Hopefully, one of them will contact the County Sheriff.

"Turn here, man." Glenn requested.

I don't see a house or a farm or anything other than corn and bean fields. We drove for about two miles until we arrived at a small acreage hidden with pine trees as a wind break from the north Iowa winter winds. It was a ranch-style white house and a two-car attached garage and a white Morton building that is about forty by thirty feet in size. The Morton building sat with closed implement and walk-in doors to the north of the residence.

The house has not been painted in forty years and has black plastic on the windows to save money for drapes. There was a broken-down riding lawn mower in the front yard that probably stopped running the last time the lawn was mowed, about a month ago. The lane to the house had weeds growing in the center with matted down rock and gravel for tire paths. The right garage door was open, and a lone pickup was parked in the visible stall. The left door must be off the tracks as it was uneven when closed. I noticed a chemical smell in the air and the constant sound of cicadas filled the late cool summer night.

As we slowly proceeded up the drive to the house, a White male with no shirt and gray sweatpants stepped out from between the pickup and the garage wall. He was smoking a cigarette, staring us down from behind his

1980s' style glasses. His sandy blonde hair was snarled, and his beard patchy and unkempt. He stood with his left hand on his hip as he took drags off his smoke.

"Stop the truck!" Glenn yelled at Pete, startling him.

Pete slammed on the brakes, and the truck came to a sliding, dusty stop.

"Wait right here. Don't get out the truck 'til I tell you." Glenn ordered.

Glenn opened the door, stepped out, and immediately raised his hands high above his head. He slid to his right, around the opened door, and walked slowly toward the man, never taking his eyes off him. He arrived at the front of the truck and stopped. The man had removed a Taurus .380 semiautomatic silver and black pistol from the small of his back and pointed at the feet of Glenn.

"You carryin'?" he shouted.

"Nope!"

"Turn 'round, lemme see."

Glenn spun slowly and looked at Pete rolling his eyes.

"Good. Come 'ere, boy." He ordered Glenn to approach while still pointing the pistol at him.

Glenn shuffled forward to the man with his hands still above his head.

"What the fuck?" I said under my breath.

"I don't like this at all," Pete replied.

I nodded my head as I watched intently checking out every movement, every motion.

I still had my Glock in my right hand and now have a hold of the inner door handle with my left. If the shooting starts, I need to get out quickly to return fire. Glenn and the man spoke to each other; not knowing what was being said, I became even more nervous. Glenn turned to us smiling uneasy and motioned for us to come to him by waving us over.

Pete turned the truck's ignition off and opened his door. I stepped out of the back and walked to the front of the truck, utilizing the body of the truck, and opened doors as cover in the event they opened fire. Cautiously... Moving...Watching...

I returned the Glock to the small of my back waistband as I cleared the front of the truck and walked adjacent to Pete. We walked about ten to twelve feet apart, so we were not as easy of a target. The man still had his gun in his hand, and judging by his fidgety movements, he was tweaking, which is not a good combination.

"Show me yer hands!" the man yelled at us.

We both held our hands out with palms up to show we were empty-handed except for the brown paper bag, which Pete was holding in his right hand.

The man had his pistol trained on Pete, then to me, then back to Pete. We stopped behind Glenn.

"See, they cool, man." Glenn expressed to the man.

Glenn held his hand out toward the man like he was introducing the next act on stage. "This is Zombie."

"What's up, man? How ya doin'?" I asked in a cool calm voice trying not to alert or spook this guy.

"How am I doin' man? How am I doin'? How tha fuck ya think I'm doin'?" He mimicked me in a sarcastic voice.

"What kind of question is that? You a cop?" he questioned, aggravated.

"What? Na, man, just bein' polite. That's all." I bargained, trying to remain calm.

"Hmmm," was his response.

"Hey, show him the bag, go 'head, show 'em," Glenn said as he stepped in front of me to Pete.

Pete opened the brown paper bag and rolled the top of the bag down, so it was easier to peer into the bag. He extended his arms toward Zombie with the bag open. Zombie looked into the bag for a moment and then smiled. That was a good sign.

"How many?" he asked, not taking his eyes out of the bag.

"One thousand, I counted 'em myself." I responded, waiting for a compliment. Nothing.

"How much you want?" Zombie questioned.

"Half."

"Hmm."

What does that mean? I thought to myself. *Too much?*

After some contemplation by Zombie, he said agreed.

He began to shift around and looked up. He held his hands up to his eyes as if he were looking through binoculars and looked out to the road, then walked toward it. He stopped for a moment and turned back to us.

"Who is that?" Zombie pointed to the road in front of his house.

I turned around and looked, scanning from left to right. Did one of the cover officers drive up the road? I continued to stare down the road, attempting to focus in the dark.

"Who is who?" I turned and asked.

"There! Drivin' on the road! Right fuckin' there!" Zombie yelled, still pointing at the road, then pointed to the sky.

"You guys bring a fuckin' choppa?"

"What the fuck is going on?" I questioned anyone who would answer, looking back and forth to the others.

By this time, Pete and Glenn were both shifting around watching each other, looking in the sky and down the road trying to see what Zombie sees. I don't see anything. Is Zombie screwing with us? Does he really see something or is he hallucinating?

"You bring the cops!" Zombie yelled at Glenn now pointing the gun at his head.

"Whoa, whoa, whoa! I didn't bring no cops! These guys are cool, man! You need to chill, man! There's no one here, just us!" Glenn began pleading for his life, literally.

Zombie turned and bolted toward the garage blindly shooting behind him. One round narrowly missing me. Glenn ran after him; I ran after Glenn. This shit just got real in an instant, and we need to apprehend Zombie before he reaches the interior of the house. Who knows what's inside there?

I caught up to Glenn as he reached the garage and bodychecked him like a hockey defender into the glass of the hockey rink. His body slamming into the tailgate, then falling to the concrete garage floor. I grabbed him by the back of the shirt and dragged him to the other side of the pickup, putting the truck between us and the walk-in door to the house that Zombie entered.

Pete followed behind me and went straight to the door and reached up and attempted to turn the doorknob. Locked… He tried again… A bullet came crashing through the wood barrier between Pete and Zombie. Then another and another. Pete dove for cover behind him toward the engine compartment of the truck. He low-crawled around the front under the bumper. He had to navigate through black plastic garbage bags filled with who knows what and empty beer cans and whiskey bottles. Doesn't this guy know how to recycle?

He made his way to the driver's side where Glenn and I were. Two more shots tore through the door and lodged in the truck's passenger side. Pete verified with me that we were all right, I nodded in response.

I drew my Glock from the small of my back and pointed it at Glenn.

"Get on yer face! Now!" I yelled at Glenn while I was maintaining cover behind the pickup.

"Whoa, dude! What the fuck is yer problem?" He responded, now fearful to move.

"Police! Stay on the ground!" I instructed in an authoritative voice.

"Holy fuck! Yer a cop? You motherfucker! I'm going to fuckin' kill you!" Glenn yelled at me, trying to roll out from under my boot that is still attached to his back.

"Shut up and get on your face! Now!" I ordered.

Pete had drawn his weapon and directed it to the door that the rounds had exited.

"Superman! Superman! Superman!" Pete shouted into the front of his hooded sweatshirt.

He had his cell phone in his left hand talking to someone briefly apprising them of the situation. As he was talking, I spotted some blood dripping from his left hand.

"Are you hit?" I asked Pete.

"What? Oh, I think I caught one in the shoulder." Pete looked himself over and found a bullet grazed his left shoulder, tearing more clothing than skin. It was probably from Zombie shooting blindly outside the garage. Pete opened and closed his hand a couple of times and outstretched his hand above his head then put it down.

"Yep, I'm good, but I'll have a battle scar," Pete said, chuckling.

Glenn's hands were in the interlocked position on top of his head, still cussing and calling me everything but White. I continued to maintain my left foot on his back with my Glock pointed at the back of his head. Rotating my head to Pete then to Glenn, then to the door and back and forth. Watching, waiting, trying to listen for sirens or confirmation of backup coming to bail us out. *Now what*, I thought.

Five more rounds exploded through the door and into our cover. Pete and I both flinched and ducked. We verified with each other our welfare. I even checked with Glenn that he was all right. "Fuck you," was his response.

"Shoot the door and let him know we're still here." I requested to Pete.

Pete, still with his weapon, pointed at the door.

"If he opens the door, I'm shooting him."

Three more shots crashed through the door. Pete returned fire, putting eight rounds into the door in a nice tight pattern. The gun smoke and deafening echo from the reports have now clouded our senses. I shook my head trying to clear the fogginess. Pete had a look of satisfaction on his face with a slight smirk as if to say, *That'll teach him to shoot at us.*

CHAPTER 7

I n the distance, we could hear the faint rhythmic sound of the police sirens getting closer. As the squad cars approached, the sirens stopped and the skidding sound of the law enforcement vehicles on the gravel road made me feel a little at ease.

Pete yelled, "In here! In here!"

The resounding sound of the officers running got closer, then I heard it, and my feeling of comfort quickly to turned to, "Oh shit!"

I heard orders being shouted, almost incoherently and in unison, "Get on the ground, drop the gun, let me see your hands, drop the gun, put the gun down!" The deputies, not knowing who I am, are pointing their handguns at me while barking orders.

I'm yelling back, pleading, "Don't shoot, I'm a cop! Don't shoot, I'm a cop!"

Pete was also yelling repeatedly at the deputies, "Don't shoot he's a cop!"

The deputies who had their Glocks directed at me were shaking so bad that if I stand still, they will probably miss me with their shots. However, I hope it does not come to that. I reached into the collar of my shirt and pulled out my badge, which is dangling from the tied green 550 cord on the black badge holder. I held it up high with my left hand, so the deputies could see I'm holding a police badge. One deputy even had his finger on the trigger and left eye closed as if he was on the training shooting range. The only thing standing between that round entering my chest cavity and staying right where it is was the five-and-half-pound trigger tension slowly decreasing every growing second.

"Stop!" Pete yelled so loud that it even startled me.

Both deputies turned to Pete.

"Put your guns down and get behind the truck. The bad guy is in the house! He's a cop!" Pete pointed at me and emphasized *He's*.

Both deputies took cover behind the truck with us. They sat on the floor next to each other with their backs against the back door of the truck sweating and panting, trying to collect themselves to understand what is going on.

I extended my right hand to the closest deputy. "Officer Phil Quick, how ya doin'?"

Smiling, trying to lessen the tension of the gun smoke-filled garage.

I borrowed a set of zip cuffs from the deputy closest to me and zip-tied Glenn's hands behind his back. While in the cover position, I patted him down for weapons, only recovered a folding knife in his right front pocket of his jeans. He won't be needing that any longer. Glenn sat Indian style on the concrete floor in what I presumed was motor oil. The smell of gunpowder and old pungent garbage from the twenty or so black-filled garbage bags in the corner of the garage overpowered us to the point that the thought of a dead body in there might be possible.

"Pete! Pete!" I called to him attempting to gain his attention.

He turned to me and raised his eyebrows with a questioning gesture.

"We need to get out of here to better cover. I got Glenn. You guys provide cover for us, then I will for you. Let me get to the truck and get my rifle." I suggested with a hint of matter of fact.

Pete nodded in approval.

I looked at Glenn and told him we are going to get up and run to the pickup truck.

His response, "Fuck you."

"Fine, but yer getting up on my three, ready? One, two... *three!*"

I grabbed Glenn under his left arm, and in one swift motion, I picked him up to his feet and forced him out through the vehicle garage door, keeping my body between Glenn and the house. My left hand on his back between his shoulder blades. When we reached the pickup, I pushed him to the ground next to the bed of the truck on the passenger side. Glenn fell to his knees, then his stomach, unable to use his hands as a cushion while they're zip-tied behind his back. He lied on his belly complaining. I told him to stay right there and not to move.

I opened the back-passenger door of the pickup and unlocked the seat back, then folded it forward. My "go bag" and rifle case were right where I left them. I restored my Glock in the small of my back waistband and threw the "go bag" on the ground at Glenn's feet, then unzipped my rifle bag. I freed my AR15 from the Velcro straps and chambered a round. The securing sound of the 5.56mm

80

round slamming into the empty chamber now occupying the space from which death arrives.

I threw the dual point sling over my head and under my left arm and flipped the covers off the four-power Trijicon ACOG (Advanced Combat Optical Gunsight) optics. Sliding to the front of the pickup behind the "A" post on the passenger side as if it were a slow dance step, I shouldered my rifle and kept a low profile using the engine block as cover and concealment.

"Pete! Pete! Now!" I called out, keeping my rifle pointed at the front door of the house.

I did not have a good angle to see the interior garage door, but if that front door opened, a rain of hot lead would be piercing the steel, wood, and Zombie.

The two deputies ran out of the bay door first to my location and slid around the front of the pickup both falling on top of each other. I instructed one to get to the back-driver's side by the tailgate to provide rear security and the other in prone behind the front tire on the passenger side. A series of gunshots ripped through the interior door of the garage from the inside of the house and entered the body of the pickup in the garage. I did not have a clear shot on the interior door, but I could put suppression fire in the wall of the garage to the right of the door.

In law enforcement, suppression fire is not allowed. We are responsible for every round that leaves the muzzle of our weapons. But as a Marine Grunt, I understand the importance of suppression fire, and I have a man inside that garage that needs to get to safety. I feel comfortable with my shooting proficiency that I know where every round impacted during my suppression fire entourage.

I fired twenty-two, 5.56mm rounds into the wall of the garage. There was a short lull. Auditory exclusion had set in. I could hear the faded echo of Pete yelling that he was coming out.

"Now!" I called out.

I fired eight more rounds into the wall, then reloaded. The empty magazine landed on the back of the deputy at my feet. Pete sprinted to the back of the pickup, barrel rolled into the bed, and then slid over the passenger side of the bed rail. He landed on Glenn with a breath-relieving thud.

"Pete! Ya good?" I yelled while still concentrating on the house.

"Ya, I think so," he responded, checking himself over, looking for bullet holes.

"Yep, good!"

The front door flew open, and a barrage of automatic gunfire erupted in the night. There are two sounds that are absolutely deafening in a gunfight. The first being the resonance of automatic gunfire at you. And the second is the sound of the firing pin falling on an empty chamber when you depress the trigger in a gunfight.

I crouched down behind the truck as the rounds impacted the sheet metal and glass, ripping through as if a hot ember through fabric. The shooting stopped. I placed the stock of my rifle into my left shoulder and fired twenty-five rounds into the door. I conducted a tactical magazine exchange and dropped the mag with five rounds onto the deputy below me. I yawned and shook my head in the attempt to open my ears back up so I can hear. I did this multiple times. Yep, I can't hear shit.

"Everyone good? Hey! We good!" I asked, trying to gain some composure during the middle of a firefight with a tweaker firing automatic weapons.

Where in the hell do they get automatic weapons?

I kept my weapon directed at the house and looked down after hearing confirmation from everyone except the deputy at my feet. I nudged his leg with my foot, nothing.

"Deputy. Deputy?" I nudged his leg again, then saw the pool of crimson liquid forming on the right side of his head.

Shit!

"Pete! He's been hit!" I pointed down at the deputy trying not to remove myself from the situation with Zombie. A calmness overtook my body as I became more heightened with clarity. At this point, I felt as if tunnel vision had set in, and everything around me was hazy except for the crystal-clear path from the magnification of my optics to the front door. This can be equated as a pitcher to the catcher's mitt in a baseball game.

Pete duckwalked to me and pulled the deputy from his final resting spot. The lifeless body of the deputy slid past me, rubbing against my support leg, smearing blood on the rock driveway in a trail about one foot wide. The thought of dying on this shithead's driveway really sucked. I looked down briefly to apologize to the young warrior. I didn't know his name, only Deputy. The somber moment turned to anger and sorrow.

The door opened again, and another series of automatic gunfire threatened us and compromised our cover. We needed to move. There was no solid glass left in the truck; all four tires were completely flat. There are bullet entry and exit holes throughout the pickup. Fluid was leaking out to the rock drive, and a small fire had started in engine compartment. The truck was destroyed.

I dropped to a squat and checked my ammo supply in my go bag. Six full AR mags and three Glock mags. I have no idea how much ammunition Zombie has, but he must have a lot, the way he's going through it. The rounds stopped impacting near us, and the sound of the gunfire shifted. I peered over my left shoulder across the hood of the truck and observed Zombie shooting out toward the bean field behind me.

This was my chance! I got to get some shots in now!

I peered through the ACOG and steadied the red chevron on the right side of Zombie's chest. Zombie had shifted his stance and had his right side facing me. My target was limited due to the angle of my position and Zombie holding up his brown wood and black metal AK-47, in a firing position, but I had to take the shot.

We are trained to fire until the threat is eliminated and aim for center mass. Center mass was not available, aim small, miss small, I thought as I recited the acronym "BRASS" in my head. BRASS stands for breath, relax, aim, squeeze, shoot, which I learned on the firing range in the Marine Corps.

I squeezed the trigger of my custom-built AR15, gasses and debris encompassing my face and blurring my vision.

The first round striking Zombie in the right forearm and the second in the right shoulder. He fell back into the house and landed on his back, then kicked the door shut. Two rounds missed and impacted the door jamb where he was standing.

What was he shooting at in the field? I turned to look over my right shoulder out to the field. I wiped my face and eyes with my gloved hand, trying to clear the sweat and debris. Beyond the field, I spotted the blue and red flashing lights in the distance. A comfort feeling came over me as I briefly smiled. I returned to overwatch the house in the event of Zombie coming back out and start shooting again.

Where in the hell did he get an automatic AK? What else does he have in there?

A quick account of the known firearms is an AK-47 and a .380 pistol. And apparently, hundreds, if not thousands of rounds. I conducted a hasty inventory on myself, six 30-round Magpul magazines for my AR and three 13-round mags for my Glock 23.

"We're going to need more guns," I said to myself as I looked down in disgust, shaking my head with the coagulating blood—a remembrance of the slain deputy at my feet.

CHAPTER 8

Pete ran down the gravel road, waving his arms above his head to tell the officers in the squad cars to stop and get back. The cars came to a skidding stop, and dust and dirt filled the air and made it even harder to see. Pete rushed up to the first squad car, wiping his eyes and trying not to inhale the dirt and dust. He told them about the situation including the downed deputy. They made arrangements to get him out of the area.

Pete made his way back by using the ditch across the road as cover. I asked him to get Glenn to safety while I hold the position until the tactical team can arrive to extract Zombie, preferably alive.

Pete and the other deputy picked Glenn up off the ground and swiftly escorted Glenn to the other law enforcement vehicles and turned him over to a police officer, whom I do not know. The police squad car then backed away in the opposite direction and removed itself from the scene.

I picked up my "go bag" with my right hand and duck-walked backward away from the now desecrated pickup, with difficulty to see through the smoke and darkness that now is providing concealment to his home. All while continuing to keep my rifle pointed at Zombie's house.

I thought to myself, *I hope Pete got the insurance on the pickup.* The humorous things that are thought of in high-stress situations. It's a coping mechanism to keep one from faltering during that situation.

I backed my way to the road and then turned toward the other officers and ran to them. The loose gravel and rock slowing me as I attempted to regain my footing. I felt like I was running sluggishly, but in actuality my speed surpassed my physical capability.

I took cover behind a squad car with Pete and two other deputies. None of us had been on the west side of Zombie's house so we had no idea what was behind the house. Other than some pine trees and a cornfield, we did not have information that could help us strategically. I advised that we need to send a couple deputies down the road to the west or have some come in from the other side and post up for rear security.

It was determined that two deputies in one car would drive around the country section to the rear of the acreage and provide security at the intersection approximately one quarter of a mile west of the acreage. If any lookie-loos show up, they can deny their entry as well as keeping containment.

All the lights had been turned off in Zombie's house, the ruined pickup sat smoldering from the small fire, his house riddled with bullet holes, but the air was quiet and still. My hearing was still faltering from the close proximity of the gunfire. The red, white, and blue lights of the squad cars illuminated the house. It has the beginnings of a scene from Afghanistan but with surrounding corn and bean fields in lieu of poppy fields and mountain ranges.

As I sat on the gravel road, law enforcement officers conversed about the situation, the slain deputy, his family, and me. A lot of the law officers on the scene did not know who I was. That was about to prove problematic in a minute.

I tried to gather my wits when an unmarked black Ford F250 pickup stopped in the middle of the gravel road. A White man in his sixties exited the truck and instantly put on his white Stetson cowboy hat with a black horsehair band and looked up. The man looked as if he stepped out of the lawman's office of an old western movie. He shook his head and mumbling something as he walked toward us. It appeared as if he was a county sheriff from the 1880s in Arizona with a large white mustache that would make Sam Elliot envious. His bowlegged gait and dusty brown leather, pointed toe cowboy boots finished off the ensemble. Oh, did I mention he had a black with pearl grips .45 Long Colt Peacemaker strapped to his belt.

Figures, I thought to myself. And then I hear it...

"Who's in charge of this clusta fuck in my county?" he bellowed in a southern accent.

Pete and I looked at each other and pointed at one another. I stood up and reached my hand down to Pete and helped him up. We walked to the sheriff with our heads down like scolded puppies as we dusted ourselves off to make us more presentable. It didn't help.

Pete spoke first. "This is our cluster fuck, sir."

"Who tha fuck gave you permission to be here? Are you too good to call ahead of time an' ask me if you could blow up my county?" the sheriff questioned.

"Sir, with all due respect, we didn't have the time to contact anyone. We didn't know that we would be here prior to us arriving. We apologize for not communicating.

We would have if we could have." Pete bargained with the sheriff for his understanding.

"You know as well as anyone that these things happen when dealing with dopers. They don't see the jurisdictional lines like us. This is an unfortunate situation and outcome, but we need to get this guy out of his house and to jail." Pete continued in his best politician imitation while looking like someone from a downtown night club in Minneapolis.

The sheriff looked back and forth at us. I'm sure we are quite a sight. I stood there with my tattered and torn blue jeans, sleeveless T-shirt, biker vest, red bandanna around my head, dirt on my face and arms, mixed with blood, sweat, and probably a little bit of pee. All with my AR rifle slung tactically across my chest. I'm sure I looked like a stunt double on the movie *Expendables* and not a police officer in Iowa.

"We need to unfuck this most 'rikki tick!' What do you two jugheads have in mind?" the sheriff, clearly a Vietnam Veteran, questioned us.

"We need to extract Zombie and secure the clan lab. We set up a deal to give him one thousand pseudo pills in exchange for product, so he's got to have a lab in there. Where's the nearest Clan Lab cleanup crew?" I offered a solution in the hopes that he would allow us to utilize his resources.

A "clan lab" is short for clandestine lab or methamphetamine manufacturing laboratory. Zombie is a meth cook and in order for us to enter the house safely, we need a special tactical team that is certified to enter meth labs. They use special personal protective equipment (PPE) and special training that not all tactical teams have. It would be approximately two hours for a Lab CERT team to assemble and arrive.

I suggested we get some snipers in place and an assault team ready in the event that Zombie launches an attack we would have a countermeasure.

"You know what your doin, boy?" the sheriff asked me.

I told him I did and could assemble an assault team if I could use some of his deputies. During this short amount of time, a few Iowa State Troopers and deputies from surrounding counties had received the information of the standoff and added to our makeshift platoon of law enforcement officers.

We made a barrier with the squad cars about a quarter of a mile east of the acreage and set up a command post where the sheriff regained command with the assistance of Pete and me. One of the troopers was a sniper on the tactical team and had all his equipment with him. He was not part of the Clan Lab Team but a marksman observer on the Special Reaction Team (SRT). I asked him where he thought his best vantage point would be. We discussed it for a few minutes, and he made a decision on location for his sniper's nest. He retrieved his gear from his squad car and took off vanishing into the night. I would not see him again until the end.

"By a show of hands, who here has tactical experience?" I asked the group of ten or so law enforcement officers.

Three guys raised their hands, all three are former Marines. I didn't know there were this many marines in law enforcement in this area. This is going to be helpful.

"Great! We have a fireteam!" A sense of relief fell over me, knowing that I have three brothers to assault this house with me.

However, there might not be a house left standing to investigate. We will cross that road when we get there. We need to get Zombie out of there quickly.

I requested a vest from anyone who had an extra, since mine is still in the destroyed pickup, which sucks because it was my favorite vest. A deputy about my size said I could use his. He retrieved it from the trunk of his car and handed it to me. I thanked him and removed my biker vest and donned the bulletproof vest that will not stop a rifle round. *Well, it's better than nothing*, I thought. I handed my colors to the deputy and asked that he keep it in a safe place. He held it up inspecting it in admiration.

"I'll need that back when we're done, brother."

He smiled and nodded.

I requested the three Marines/deputies to assemble on me off to the side of the hasty command post in the ditch of the country road. Two of the deputies sat on a metal drainage pipe that ran under the entrance road to the bean field. I didn't have access to a handheld police radio, but one of the deputies did. I heard radio traffic and people speaking along with distant sirens. Ambulances and firetrucks had been requested and were starting to arrive. They were told to stay on the blacktop a mile and a half away and wait. Let's see if they listen.

As we congregated in the ditch introducing ourselves and making a hasty op order, an onslaught of automatic gunfire erupted in the night. Bullets impacting into the vehicles and ground around us. The hissing of the bullets and snaps of the close shots made us take cover in the ditch. I looked at the three deputies, all of which were smiling. I smiled and shook my head. The shooting ended.

"Anyone hit?" I yelled.

"Everyone check each other!" I heard someone holler, unsure who it was.

"Good!"

"Good!"

"Good!"

And more, "Good." Repeated in the ditch. No one was hit, thank God.

"Who's in contact with the sniper?" I asked the group at the command post.

"I am." Another trooper raised his hand and stepped forward.

"Ask him what he sees and if he can get a shot off if Zombie sticks his head out." I requested.

"Will do," he responded.

A few seconds later, the trooper stepped to me and said, "He does have a shot, but the first auto gunfire was directed at him, and he had to get skinny."

That tells me Zombie has NVGs (night vison goggles) or thermal imaging.

Shit, that's not good.

I checked with the command post what the ETA (estimated time of arrival) is on the lab team. The sheriff told me under two hours.

With the continuing threat that Zombie presents, we made an executive decision to assault the residence. The sheriff was very apprehensive as we, Pete and I, have already made a mess. But with the growing problem with the "Tango" having an unknown quantity of automatic weapons, and the willingness to use them, the decision became clear what we needed to do.

CHAPTER 9

The makeshift fireteam consisted of all four of us former Marines. Bryan, a tall lanky White guy with brown short hair, did two tours in Iraq and was shot twice and blown up once. He has three Purple Hearts and other various valor medals to add to his accolades. He was also a firearms instructor for his unit.

Alex, a half-Hispanic, half-White guy with his tatted sleeves on both arms, was a fitness machine. He did one tour in Iraq before getting shot once in the chest. He made a slow full recovery and decided to get out. This guy can run forever and still runs four to eight miles a day.

And Lynne. Lynne is a bad dude. He is about six foot one inch and 225 pounds of ripped steel. Lynne is Native American and incredibly intelligent. He was deployed to Iraq, Afghanistan, and a few other places that I can't disclose as a HUMINT ops guru, which means he reads and dissects people. He was awarded the highest medal awarded for valor for saving the lives of three Marines in mission in some unnamed country.

I could not have assembled a better fireteam to assault the likes of Zombie. Maybe when this is all over, we can sit down and tell war stories, drink beer, and grill steak, which I will gladly provide.

My fireteam and I made our way west in the ditch using the shadows and unmowed weeds as cover. I assigned myself as the team leader and point man. This is usually not the case with the team leader position, but since I'm the most familiar with the area and the details of the house and property, I took it upon myself to take point. All the while knowing that my wife is due in a few months with my first child.

This added more pressure after I had a little bit of time to contemplate the future of my daughter, with or without me. I needed to vacate the thoughts and images of my not-yet-born child.

Focus!

I internally battled the emotions of a soon-to-be father and brought myself back to the situation at hand.

Focus!

If I don't concentrate, not only will my daughter not get to meet her father, but my fireteam's lives will be at risk as well.

We crouched and walked with exaggerated step after step, heel, toe.

Heel, toe.

Stop, listen.

Heel, toe, heel, toe.

Stop, listen, observe.

We moved in cover formation with Lynne as rear security scanning back every other step.

Our fireteam all donned AR15s with various optics. I was the only one with an ACOG; the other deputies had Eotech holograph red dots. The fortunate thing with Marines/deputies as my fireteam is, we all know the basics of weapons, tactics, and assault missions. There was no time to learn. It was a game of follow the leader and assault the house. The only difference is, now we can't blow a hole in the side of the building and shoot anyone standing.

We are law enforcement, and we need to keep in mind that we are responsible for every round that exits the muzzle of our weapons. No more spray and pray. Yes, our military training is going to help with the stress level and suppressing the anxiety, but we need to apprehend Zombie and keep him alive for trial. I did remind the fireteam of this distinction, which they apprehensively agreed.

We did not have access to NVGs or thermals, but at my command, all the spotlights on the squad cars will be trained on the house in the expectations of blinding Zombie and make our assault more proficient.

We proceeded past the residence in the ditch, with our rear security covering the front door area. Once we successfully cross the road, he will join us. But crossing a danger zone, we need the security that the other officers and their location cannot provide. I crossed the road first and made my way to a tree adjacent to the side of the garage. I fell to my left knee with my rifle trained on the front of the garage. All I could see was the face of the garage and only knew the right door was still open.

Once I arrived safely, I signaled with a whistle and a wave for the next deputy to cross. He crossed the road and found a tree to my left and got into the deadly ready prone position that Marines are naturally accustomed to, leg cocked in and feet flat against the ground, so the heels are not exposed. Using the magazine as a bipod and lying as flat as humanly possible, peering through the holograph sight.

The next one crossed, quickly, crouching and running. He slid to a stop next to the other deputy like he was sliding into second base legging out a double. He turned his weapon toward the back of the garage while in the kneeling position.

The deputy in the rear security position had blended into the ditch well enough. I am not exactly sure of his position. I whistled and waved. Nothing. I whistled and waved again. Nothing. I looked down at the deputy in the prone position. He shrugged his shoulder with bewilderment. I looked back at the ditch, trying to scan the area as my eyes have adjusted to the darkness. The deputy then popped up in front of me and crouched/walked to me from about twenty feet away. How the hell did he cross without us seeing him?

He low-crawled from his position across the road to ours without us seeing him. I smiled and shook my head. He took a knee behind me, put his back against mine, and pointed outboard. Good Marine!

I could feel the heat of the burning undercover pickup that was about forty feet away from us. The glow of the fire and smell of burning plastic, rubber, and fabric filled the cool late summer air. The breeze had shifted and blew the smoke and odor into us. It did not phase the deputies as they held their position awaiting orders.

As I contemplated our next move, I took everything in with the Marines-turned-proficient law enforcement officers willing to do what it takes to complete the mission.

Ten hours ago, when they started their shift, getting ready to drive the back roads and highways of the county and provide the security and safety for locals and visitors alike. The last thing they thought about doing was a full-blown assault on a house against a meth head with an automatic AK-47. Oh, the wonderments of law enforcement, everyday different from the last and the next.

I knew that we can get to the interior of the garage without being seen by skirting along the front of the garage bay door. If the interior door is barricaded, we won't be able to get in and then we're stuck until the clan lab team arrives. We didn't have a ram or a shield. Should we? Yes, but we didn't. The lab team was still about one more hour out. The trooper sniper had our overwatch position protected. We made a collective agreement to attempt the interior door. Lynne held up an object in his left hand. I reached out for it, and he pulled his hand away.

"What is that?" I whispered.

"Shape charge."

I chuckled.

Good Marine.

That will help us get into the garage door.

"On me." I ordered the deputies to follow me to the inside of the garage.

We will be in a compromising position, but we have the pickup for cover as well as the improper angles of attack. Lynne handed the shape charge to Alex. I moved to the front of the garage, into the door, and set up a secure position behind Zombie's pickup. I signaled the next deputy. Then the next. Finally, the rear security deputy. All the while, my rifle pointed at the walk-in door.

Alex made his way to the door and began to place the shape charge on the doorknob and the hinges. He had removed the protective coverings of the explosives as he was moving to the door. This is a technique practiced, not picked up on the fly. By placing the explosives on the door, he was in a very compromising position in front of the door. He knew this and precisely placed the charges anyways. This is not a new experience for these guys, just in Iowa and not Iraq or Afghanistan.

Once the explosive devices were in place, Alex made his way to cover behind the truck.

"On me," Alex quietly said as he held the control device ready to discharge the explosives.

I nodded in approval.

"Fire in the hole!" he shouted so all could hear.

Booom!

The door blew inward with a deafening explosion with debris and shrapnel flying in every direction. We rushed up the two steps with our ears ringing through the smoke of the explosives and the smoke of the truck intertwining to gates of the fog of war.

We made our way through the door in file cover formation and began to clear the first room we encountered, the kitchen. Lynne stayed at the garage doorway and posted up facing down the basement stairwell. Our assault team passed the basement stairwell as we entered the kitchen. We needed to clear the house before we link back up with Lynne.

To say the kitchen was a mess was an understatement. Old rotten remnants of food on plates, in bowls, in old rusty pans, and on any flat surface, cluttered the preparing area. Old still folded newspapers stacked two feet high covered the dining table with a single chair occupying the dining area. Black fifty-five-gallon plastic garbage bags piled six feet high, blocking the sliding glass door to the outside. The stench of rotted food overpowered the smell of smoke from outside. Oh, what I would do for an SCBA right now!

There was no path through the kitchen garbage littered the floor, so stepping cautiously was paramount. Steady footing would be a luxury. We made our way through the "kitchen of a thousand corpses" and pressed forward to the living room.

I was the first to encounter the living room. Imagine, if you will, the worst living room you have ever been in and then multiply that by ten. How anyone could live in this disorder is beyond me. A one-foot path from the entrance to the one cushion on the couch. Clothes and rags of every type strewn about like a tornado had gently, strategically placed each article in the room.

A stack of obsolete televisions on the opposite wall of the couch encompassed the wall along with broken and disassembled electronic devices. Scratched off stolen lottery tickets in neat piles on the floor next to the couch. Posters and cut-out pictures from nudie magazines filled every vacant space on the walls, windows, tabletops, cupboards, and ceiling—yes ceiling. And the pictures that didn't make the cut stayed in the stacks of porno mags piled on the chairs.

Flies have found our location and conducted their own assault. I do my best to contain my composure and not make sudden movements of fly swatting.

I took cover on the right-side interior wall while Bryan posted up on the opposite side from me. Weapons pointed down the hall in anticipation of the automatic 7.62 rounds to start ripping through the sheetrock and wood that separates us from certain death.

"Moving," I announced.

I stepped forward and approached the first doorway on the right. I J-hooked right and cleared the small bedroom. I could not get the door all the way open due to the debris behind the door. The parts of lawnmowers and toolboxes filled the room. Random tools and auto parts encompassed the uncarpeted floor. This is where he works on his machinery, the bedroom? I shook my head in disbelief.

"Clear! Coming out!" I called out.

There was no reason to be quiet since we used explosive devices to gain entry. I'm sure he knew we were here.

I reentered the hallway and fell in behind the other two deputies. They moved forward through the hallway in unison and with the likeness of a well-oiled machine. Weapon-mounted tactical flashlights guiding their way through the smoke, haze, and darkness.

The next room on the left, the door got booted open by Bryan.

"Good Lord! Shut the door now!" I yelled, covering my nose and mouth. The smell of a full toilet and something presumably dead overtook us and made me throw up in the middle of the hallway.

Bathroom. Clear(ish). We will need to come back and check that's not a body of a person in there.

Next room, I turn the doorknob and push the door open.

Bedroom.

Seriously?

A made bed with the corners and edges crisply tucked. A dresser with family pictures in frames, multiple prescription pill bottles, a half-full bottle of water, a digital watch, and a handkerchief. A neat pile of folded clothes on a sitting chair to the left of the bed. A reading lamp and a book between the bed and chair. The closet had clothes hung up in color order from light to dark, left to right. The carpet looked relatively new and freshly vacuumed. I haven't seen a vacuum.

What the fuck? was all I could think.

Clear!

I stood in a tactical position at the door jamb of the final bedroom. The two deputies fell in behind me. I felt the hand on my left shoulder gave a squeeze, indicating they were ready to move. We made our way to the basement entrance and connected with the rear security deputy. This whole process took less than two minutes.

"Friendly!" I called out so Lynne would know not to shoot.

"Any movement?" I asked.

He shook his head two times to indicate no. His cheek welded to the shoulder stock as if it were a part of him. A Marine and his weapon is the most dangerous thing on earth.

With the light from the weapon illuminating the stairwell, I noticed the blood smear on the wall in three different spots at about shoulder high. This confirmed my query of hitting him with a round. I pointed to the blood so that all were on the same page that we were dealing with a wounded, drug-induced man.

I patted the top of my head to indicate "on me." Then shuffled to the top step and exchanged positions with Lynne. I stepped down and began to cautiously move forward down the steps into the unknown. This is a dangerous position, the fatal funnel, if you will. Stairwells are extremely dangerous and need to be vacated quickly.

With the unknown that we are strolling into my senses on heightened awareness—sounds amplified, tunnel vision setting in, and lactic acid burning the muscles. Once I reached the last step, I J-hooked to the right, and Alex behind me J-hooked to the left. I went to the right because I am a naturally left-handed long gun shooter. The other deputies with me are all right-handed.

This helps to know as one is clearing a building with the proper technique, "Wall, body, weapon," which translated means that as you are standing by a wall, door, or window, the placement needs to be your weapon furthest from the wall. For example, if the wall is on my right, I want my body between the wall and my weapon. Then shoulder my rifle in my left shoulder. This way, peering around a door while "slicing the pie," I make my body less of a target, and the muzzle of my weapon is the first thing the target sees and presumably the last.

As I entered the dark room, I instantly inhaled a horrible chemical smell mixed with urine and feces that burned my nostrils and lungs. I found multiple tables with glass bottles, bags, tubes, canisters of chemicals, and powder. A dark green five-gallon bucket used as a makeshift toilet positioned in the far corner with the buzz of hundreds of flies. Fire burns and spray-painted symbols and crude sayings riddle the cinder block walls encasing the makeshift laboratory. The scene looked like the mixture of a chemistry lab from a 1940s *Frankenstein* movie and the basement from the *Blair Witch Project*.

A dim, flickering single lightbulb attempted to illuminate the room. I felt a hand on my shoulder and a squeeze. I had placed my right hand over my mouth and nose and turned to Alex. I did not want to puke again. He pulled me back and toward the other two deputies on the left side of the stairwell. I fell into the stack they had formed on a dark hole in the ground about three by three feet with a wooden ladder leading down to the abyss.

"Who's first?" I asked, knowing good and well that it was me.

There was no way I was letting these guys go before me. This was my mess, and I couldn't let another one die. Lynne extended his non-weapon hand to me. He nudged my arm with his hand. I looked down and opened my hand to receive the object he was holding. A flash-bang. Yes! This guy is getting a case of beer when we're done with this. Actually, they all will be. Beer, Scotch, steaks, hell, whatever they want.

I told him since he brought it, he could throw it. He reached into his vest pouch and pulled out another flash-bang and said he had more. Oh, this is too good!

"I'll throw the first one, wait ten seconds, then throw the next one." I instructed.

A flash-bang is a distraction device that is both very loud and very bright, hence the name "flash-bang." It operates the same as a grenade. You pull the safety pin, let the spoon fly, and then throw it toward your desired direction. It disorients the target for enough time to launch an assault. By throwing one, waiting, then throwing another, this confuses said bad guy. But when there is only one way in and one way out, it makes it more confusing. In this case, Zombie with automatic weapons, it will draw the fire to the opening, then when the second one goes off, it will distract him enough that I can drop in and shoot him. Or it may not work, who knows.

The deputy pulled the pin and tossed the flash-bang down the hole at an angle to the direction of the tunnel. Three seconds later...

Boooom!

We were ready for it, so we closed our eyes and covered our ears the best we could. However, in a tunnel this size and not prepared for it, it will be deafening and blinding. I waited fifteen seconds and then tossed mine down the hole, three seconds later...

Boooom!

As soon as it went off, I dropped into the hole and stooped down with my rifle in the ready position pointing down the tunnel. My tactical light tried to cut through the smoke but no luck. I moved forward enough for the next deputy to come down. He grabbed my left shoulder and squeezed. I moved forward with him in my hip pocket. We paused, one more deputy dropped in and stacked up on us. Lynne stayed on rear security up top.

We followed the one-hundred-foot tunnel to the end where we located a wooden door. The tunnel was about five feet tall and three-and-a-half feet wide. This made it a tight fit with all our gear on and having to crouch low while being careful of booby traps and other debris and garbage.

The door was not secured, and there were no visible intact spiderwebs connected, which means someone has used this recently. I was unable to locate exposed wires or any explosive devices. A small glimmering light at the bottom of the door indicated a light on the other side. Alex and Bryan hugged the wall on the opposite side of the opening, preparing for the ambush on the other side. I switched arms and shouldered my rifle in my right arm so I could reach with my left hand and turned the doorknob slowly until I knew the latch bolt released form the strike.

At this point, there are a few things going through one's mind. One, it was booby-trapped and was going to explode, and since we are in a tunnel, the blast will be concentrated toward us and kill us. Two, there is an ambush waiting for us as soon as we step through; Zombie will open up with his automatic AK-47 and kill us all. Or three, nothing.

Come on number three!

I flung the door open as hard as I could and waited... nothing. I held it open with my left boot. I peered around the door to the right as well as I could. With the lights from the squad cars, I could see a body on the path to the Morton building about fifty feet from our location. I shined my light at the body, hoping and praying it was not one of us. I could see a metal object lying on the ground next to the body and shiny liquid forming on the ground. With my weapon pointed at the body, I looked back at the deputies. They also had a confused, concerned look on their face.

"You, on me." I pointed to Alex.

Bryan knew to stay in his position.

With my rifle pointed at the object and the deputy on my six, we moved forward in unity, step for step. My eyes scanning to the left and right, down and up. As I got closer, I realized what I was looking at, the body of Zombie. His AK-47 on the ground with the muzzle pointing to my left. Did he shoot himself?

What the hell?

"Friendly, coming out!" came from the bean field to my right.

I instinctively turned to my right with my weapon in the ready position.

"Who's there? Identify yourself!" I called out.

"Trooper Smythe," was the response.

The trooper sniper holding his black scoped .308 rifle inside his crossed arms, like he just shot a prized elk.

"One shot through the engine block," he said smiling, with great accomplishment.

I knelt down and inspected the limp body of Zombie and checked his pulse, nothing. His eyes open and staring into nothingness. A small round hole about the size of a dime with a dark discoloration ring one inch above his left temple. A hole the size of a golf ball indicating the exit of the well placed .30 caliber round fired by the marksman observer. Brain matter, skull fragments, and dark crimson blood entwined with the overgrown weeds and gravel.

The smoke, the sounds, the lights, the smells, the aches and pains all present but ignored.

We stood over his lifeless body, somber but content.

It's over.

CHAPTER 10

I was on patrol one spring night when I saw a White male riding a BMX bike through the city park. It was about two thirty in the morning and the park was closed. The park was a typical small-town Iowa park with a little kid's playground area with outdated equipment that sat in a weed-infested sand and rock area. There was a small cinder block building that was big enough for a two-stall bathroom. The streetlight over the playground area flickered and has been like that for the last two years.

There was no sidewalk, just walking paths from the "tweakers" cutting through the park to get to the apartment complex that primarily houses dopers. I drove adjacent to him until he got to the street. As I approached him, I activated my emergency lights and stopped him. He came to a skidding stop and spun toward me, putting his hands to his eyes to guard them from the flashing red and blue lights.

I did not recognize him at all. He was a short White male in his midtwenties. He wore a dark blue Hurley hoodie and torn-up, stained jeans. I saw the dark-colored clip of a knife in his right front jean's pocket. I introduced myself to him and asked for some identification.

He claimed he didn't have any.

I asked him where his wallet was.

"At home."

"Where's your home?"

He pointed behind me.

"What's your name?"

"Timmy."

This dance went on for a while. The local dopers know to answer each question with very little information. They think that it annoys the officers and they let them go. That is somewhat true, it does annoy us.

"Look, Timmy, I don't get off work until eight in the morning, so if you want to continue with this bullshit, I have nowhere else to be," I explained, now starting to get annoyed.

While talking with Timmy, I noticed he was becoming fidgety. He could not stand still, and he began to look beyond me checking for avenues of escape. He put his hand in a pocket and then took it out. He did this a couple of times before I stopped him.

"Timmy, stop moving around. Put both hands in your pocket and make fists with your hands. Don't take them out until I tell you to do so, understand."

Timmy shoved both hands in the front pockets of his jeans.

"Fine," he said with disgust, "Timmy Lewis, date of birth 1-20-1985. I live at 331 South First Street with my grandma."

"See, that wasn't so hard, was it?"

As I jotted everything down in my notebook, I knew I committed a rookie mistake; I did not take the knife off him before conducting the field interview. *Dumbass*, I thought to myself, *those are the mistakes that get officers killed.*

I asked him to hand me the knife. At that time, he took his right hand out of his right front pocket and pulled out a cheap, black plastic folding knife with a three-and-a-half-inch blade. I secured it in my right cargo pocket and told him to empty his pockets. He hesitated and asked why.

I explained to him, "In my experience, when someone has one weapon, they usually have another."

He rolled his eyes and reluctantly began to empty his pockets; a Nokia cell phone; two Bic lighters; loose change and a crumpled five-dollar bill; a pack of Marlboro Lights, which was opened; headphone ear buds; another set of ear buds; a phone charger; and loose pieces of paper; and of course, another folding knife.

I looked in the pack of cigarettes and moved the foil and found what I was looking for, a small baggie of meth. The typical location of small uses of meth is commonly kept behind the back row of cigarettes between the foil and the box. The smarter ones keep it under the foil in the bottom of the box, so we have to use a little more effort to find the contraband.

It was only a half gram, but it was enough to charge him with possession with the enhancement since he is in the city park. In Iowa, possession of methamphetamine is a serious misdemeanor under Code of Iowa Section 124.401(5). With the enhancement, since he is in a city park, he could get extra time, extra fine, or community service if convicted.

During a field interview of a subject, which is what this was at the time, we as police officers are taught in the academy to stand in an "interview stance" or bladed stance. This simply means in a tactical stance so that our gun side is away from the subject, so it's more difficult for them to reach for it if they were to launch an attack while standing with them. This also allows the officer to sidestep out of the way if an attack is launched from the front.

For example, my sidearm is on my right hip, my right foot would be slightly back to the rear as I'm standing, and my hands are to the front of my belt and not in my pockets.

I reached for my cuffs on the left side of my belt and as soon as I did that, Timmy took off running to my right. I don't know why he went to my right instead of turning and running away from me. A little-known fact, which is hard to tell by my stature, is I am not fast. I am much stronger than I am fast.

I reached to my right and grabbed ahold of his hoodie and would have gotten a fifteen-yard penalty for a horse-collar tackle. But I was the referee, and Timmy was going to jail. His feet came out from under him and flew above his head as he landed on his back. The air quickly left his body in a forceful thud on the ground. The soft wet grass somewhat cushioned his fall, but the fight was quickly extinguished.

I flipped him over to his belly and put both hands behind his back, then put my handcuffs on him. I stood over him with an accomplished expression on my face, but in actuality, it really wasn't that big of a deal. He's a small guy at five feet, seven inches and 160 pounds, and I'm six feet and 240 pounds.

I gathered Timmy up and walked him over to my squad car. While we walked, he pleaded with me to let him go. He just had a son and can't go to jail.

I asked him why he was using meth.

He said, breathing heavy, "It's to help me work cuz I need to stay awake."

I told him I understand the long hours and tough job at night, but I don't need meth and someone his age shouldn't either.

Timmy then said what I wanted to hear.

"Look, if ya lemme go, I will give ya anyone you want. I know a lotta dealers around here."

And now we have reached the bargaining stage.

I entertained the idea with Timmy and asked, "You can give me the guy that sold you the meth?"

He nodded his head as he looked away.

I stepped in front of him and said again, "You can and will give me your dealer?"

He looked up at me and said, "Yes."

Before I opened the car door, I asked Timmy where he got the bike.

He smiled and said it was his cousin's bike.

"Oh, what's your cousin's name? I'll make sure he gets it back." Knowing good and well he has no idea where that bike belongs.

"I can't remember his name," he said with a devilish grin.

"How 'bout that," I said as I opened the car door to my 2000 Chevrolet Lumina squad car and assisted him into the back seat.

Instead of driving directly to the jail, I took him to the police department. In Iowa, like many other states, the small-town police have to take their prisoners to the county seat, which is where the county jail is. My jail was about twelve miles away, so we went to the police department instead. A few months ago, I bolted a steel ring to my desk where I could attach a handcuff to a prisoner while I debrief them. It works well for what it is. I saw it on a movie once and thought it was a good idea.

We entered my police department office through the door off the alley where there is a parking spot designated for police only. However, during the day, everyone conducting business at city hall thinks their vehicle is more important than the police cars, so they park there to eliminate walking across the parking lot.

I escorted Timmy to my office and had him sit in the chair next to my desk. I then handcuffed him to my cuff ring.

"Do you think I'm going to run?"

I chuckled and said, "Well, you tried once."

My police department was a three-man department, so we have three desks. The chief's desk is an "L" shape, and the other two are old small gray metal desks. The evidence lockers are exactly that, lockers. I think we got them from the locker room at the high school before the remodel twenty years ago. A police scanner rests on the far corner on my desk that only picks up four channels. The main door enters into the lobby of City Hall. If there are five people in this office, it gets real small real fast.

I retrieved the confidential informant (CI) paperwork from my file cabinet. I custom made these forms after attending the Drug Enforcement Administration Basic Narcotic Training that year. It was the first training evolution in Iowa that the DEA taught. It was a two-week school that taught everything from drug identification to undercover operations to pharmacology. It was a good school that has helped me with numerous narcotic operations.

In the movies and on TV, the cops make it look so easy to set up drug buys. They talk to their informants and then go and buy the drugs in a shady part of town or in the middle of a parking lot, then bust the bad guys. Unfortunately, it is not that easy at all. This will be the beginning of exceedingly long and tedious times with someone who needs a shower and a new change of clothes. The longer he sits in my office, the fouler it gets. I need to find a candle.

The paperwork is one thing that is not portrayed accurately in the movies. Paperwork is extremely important in police work. When the investigation is over, and you have arrested a crime syndicate and now you are in court, one little slip up with the paperwork and the yearlong investigation that you've devoted your life, career, and relationships with has just gone down the shitter.

Just because you forgot to log the right amount of money or didn't have the right information on a search warrant, the case gets dismissed. I can assure you, from experience, it fucking sucks! We learn from our mistakes, hopefully, and move forward. But sometimes, those mistakes eat at you for a while, and some people lose confidence in your ability.

As Timmy squirmed in his chair, I got all my paperwork in order so we could go through it and not miss anything. I'm not going to bore you with all the details in the paperwork but to give you an idea of what is entailed; eight pages of confidential informant information, four pages of the police report, two pages of money to be used, request forms for "buy" money, request for lab forms, county attorney request forms, etc.

Now for the fun part...

"Timmy, tell me what ya know an' don't leave anything out. If ya want these charges to go away, you need to provide information that will lead to at least three arrests. Otherwise, the deal is off the table and we're done, and you go to jail. Get it?"

"Ya, I get it, dude."

"I'm gonna stop ya right there before we go any further, an' I'm going to say this as nice as I possibly can. You call me 'dude' one more time, and I'm going to kick that fucking chair over with you in it, dude."

He smiled and said sorry, which kind of surprised me, but I think I got the point across.

"So, talk to me." I sat back in my fake brown leather swivel chair.

"Okay, so I get my shit from a guy named Mikey. Mikey lives up north in Hastings. He moves a lot of shit. I don't know where he gets it, but whenever I meet with him, he has white and green. I've never met with him, and he not have some."

"White being meth, and green is weed?" I asked to clarify.

"Yes, good you're catching on."

I'm going to punch this kid before this is all over, I thought to myself.

"Mikey an' his twin brother, Jeremy, live in the traila park north of town. They been slingin' for years from their garage. They throw some awesome parties, man, ya should see some of the shit that goes on in there. I could tell ya some stories."

"What's their last name?"

"Ummmm, I dunno," he said, scratching his ratty head. He shifted in his chair and scratched his crotch.

"How do ya not know?"

"It's never come up, and I never asked. But you can ask any cop in town who the twins are, and they know 'em. They been arrested a thousand times."

"Okay, I will. So, let me ask you this, Timmy, how well do you know them? Can you buy shit from them anytime? Do you need an appointment? Can you just stop by? Explain to me how this works with the twins?"

"Man, I just stop by an' get whatever I want anytime. I bought a lot of shit from them and they don't care."

My mind was going a hundred miles an hour, thinking about how we can play this. This could be the big break that I need, this could be my big bust that every cop dreams of, and I have to rely on Timmy, fantastic.

"Timmy, will they sell to me?"

"Maybe, ya, I think they would. Why do you ask?"

"Well, you're going to introduce me to them so I can buy some dope from them. How does that sound?"

The next eight months are going to be very interesting.

CHAPTER 11

Timmy and I met in the furthest part of the cemetery on the northeast side of town. This will be the first meeting outside the time that we initially met in the park. The cemetery is not big, but it has many evergreen trees, which will help conceal our meet. I have a Sable brown, 1976 Ford F100 pickup that is primarily used to take garbage to the dump or haul leaves and wood. However, it will turn out to be a primary piece of equipment for the undercover operations for the months to come.

My pickup was dirty brown, regular cab, and two-wheel drive. It has a four-speed transmission with a "granny" low and a 302 V8 motor transplanted from a 1998 Ford Mustang. I could get the tires to smoke when prompted.

Timmy arrived on his bike—I presume his bike. I actually did not ask because I didn't want to know the answer. He hopped into the passenger side of my truck.

"Timmy, throw your bike in the back, we're goin' for a ride."

"Where we goin' boss," Timmy asked apprehensively.

"You been usin' today, Timmy?"

"No, sir, I ain't used in days since you took all my shit."

"Good, let's go."

After Timmy threw the bike in the bed of my truck, I followed the white rock trail back to the black top county road. As we bounced and jarred on the uneven road with Garth Brooks playing on the local country radio station, I glanced at Timmy to see if I could see anything that stood out such as sweat or fidgeting or any sign that would indicate that he was not up for this challenge.

"Put yer seatbelt on," I ordered before we got on the blacktop.

Timmy complied without hesitation.

"So, explain ta me how this works with yer boys in Hastings."

Timmy shifted in his seat and turned toward me on the old bench seat.

"So, it's like this. I go to their trailer and knock on the door. They answer and I ask for some white or green," Timmy stated without hesitation.

I waited for more.

"Wait, that's it?" I asked as I turned to him.

"Yep, that's it."

"Then they jus' hand it to you, and ya leave? Do they make you use it with them or in front of them?"

"Nope, not since the first time."

"It can't be that simple. There's got to be more to it. What aren't you telling me?"

I felt like this was going to be harder than it should be, and I started to get annoyed.

"How much do you pay for half gram?"

"Forty," Timmy replied without hesitation.

"What about a gram? An eight ball? Half ounce? Ounce?" I requested the information so I could jot it down in my mental notebook.

"Ounce! You think I'm a fuckin' junkie?"

"Have you not ever bought an ounce?"

"Hell, I've never bought a ball." Timmy tried to justify his usage, with small amounts to make me feel like he is an upstanding young meth user.

"If you were to buy a ball, what would they think?"

"These dudes are paranoid. They shady as shit an' they don't like anyone but their buddies and money."

"Okay, so they like money, good. I can work with that."

"What do you mean?" Timmy asked legitimately puzzled.

"So, here's how it's going to go down."

I had to talk louder because we had the windows down, and the wind was blowing through the cab of the truck. I turned down the music to aid in not having to repeat myself.

"You're gonna introduce me to these fellas as yer cousin from Des Moines. Imma biker an' my old supplier got pinched and is outta the picture. I need a new supplier to hook up my brothers for the rallies an' runs. At first, I'm going to get a small amount, have it checked, and if its good shit, I'll get more. This is a job interview for them, not me. The more shit they can get me, the more money they're gonna make. By the time this is done, I'll be buying kilos off them. If they can get weed, I want that, too. Guns, can they get me guns?" I explained this all to Timmy while driving slowly down the county road.

I was watching the road, glancing in and out of the ditches, watching for vehicles behind me. I did not get a response from Timmy.

"Hey, you payin' attention?" I snapped, turning to him.

120

"Ummm, ya I can do that. Man, you really been thinkin' about this. You want guns, too?"

"Hell ya, I want guns! As many as I can get! This has to look legit. I want as much shit as I can get, remember, this is for my brothers in the club," I said, lowering my voice to share the sincerity of my actions.

"Yer starting to not sound like a cop. I'm a little more scared now than I was, man," Timmy stated with faltering voice.

"Good. It's working."

CHAPTER 12

Being an undercover operative, one must be able to blend in. By blending in, think about your target audience, i.e., who are you buying dope from. My UC persona was a biker. When people see bikers, they think of Harleys, dopers, dirty, cussing, rude, and fighting. I transformed myself into just that.

When I first met my confidential informant (CI), I was a clean-cut police officer with no visible tattoos; a Marine style high and tight haircut, trimmed goatee. I looked, walked, talked, and acted like a Marine and a police officer.

How do I change this? First, the hair. I obviously do not have time to grow it out, so let's shave it off. Facial hair does not grow fast either, but I'll let it grow and not shave anymore; dirty stubble doesn't look cop like. I used to have my left ear pierced. I can still see somewhat of a hole. I'll shove a hoop through it and see how that looks.

Now for my clothes. I need some sleeveless Harley T-shirts to show off the guns; a long underwear shirt; black leather vest; dirty, holey jeans; and black biker boots. I went to my closet, found multiple black Harley T-shirts and cut the sleeves off. I found an old off-white long underwear shirt, some old Levi's 501 jeans, and a pair of black Georgia steel-toed work boots. I put on the ensemble and stood in front of the mirror. What was missing? Yep, too clean.

I looked like I should be in a Harley catalog and not in biker magazine. How do I change this? I took the clothes and boots off and went out to my garage. I put the clothes on the floor and began to rub dirt and grease on them all over, smearing the grease and grime into the fabric, rubbing them on the floor, hitting them on the concrete, tearing them in random places. All while listening to Guns N' Roses. The "Appetite for Destruction" album, not that "Spaghetti Incident" bullshit.

I inspected my work by holding each one up; nope, still not dirty enough. I put the clothes and boots under each tire of my truck, climbed in and started it up. I backed over the clothing and then drove forward, backed up, then forward. I did this for about five minutes. I checked out the clothing and boots. Now we're getting there!

Jewelry is an odd thing for me to wear. I do not normally wear jewelry. I need to get some silver rings, a necklace or two with a medallion or a cross, maybe a bracelet and a watch. I like to wear a watch, but I don't want to wear my good watch, so I need to find one that I don't care about. Where can I find these items?

I contacted a biker friend of mine about forty-five minutes away and gave him a list of things that I need. He told me he has everything I need.

"A black leather vest in XXL?" I asked on the phone.

"Yep, got it."

Mitchell is an old school biker and has a leather repair shop in a small town in central Iowa. He travels all over the United States to bike rallies and swap meets in a school bus painted blue and converted into a camper/storefront to sell his services. He is very talented and can make a vest and chaps in about a day in any color leather. He can add stitching and designs, pockets, and hidden storage.

I drove to his shop that afternoon. His shop is an old brick factory building with the original business name sign still up. A blue "Mitchell Leather & Canvas" sign below it with the phone number written in faded white paint. I walked up the loading dock ramp to the front door. I peered through the filthy window before I knocked on the steel door. He keeps it locked when he's not open for business because he also resides there. I don't think its zoned for residential, but he doesn't care. A few moments later, the door opened.

"Mitchell, how the hell are you?" I asked, extending my right hand to shake his.

His big meat hook grabbed a hold of my hand and pulled me in for a bro hug. Mitchell was a large dude, about six foot two and 265 pounds, depending on how much beer he drank the night before. He was about ten years older than me, and has salt and pepper hair pulled back into a ponytail of about eight inches; his beard is thick and can barely see his mouth until he laughs.

Mitchell's laugh is boisterous and very recognizable. You could hear his laugh from the other side of the room and tell it's Mitchell. And he laughs at everything, especially his own jokes. It's not that they're funny, it's funny to hear and see Mitchell laugh and then you start laughing. His laugh is contagious. He is incredibly crude and has no filter, but that's what makes Mitchell, Mitchell.

"Okay, so I found a few items you might be interested in," he said as we walked to a small room off the main showroom.

He had laid out numerous items all in order from rings to bracelets to necklaces. I requested silver, but he added some black ones in there as well. As I perused over all the jewelry items, Mitchell began telling me a biker story. I was only half listening to him as I was concentrating on the perfect accessories to my biker role. I tried on some rings and found a few that fit. I picked two bracelets and three necklaces. I asked him how much for all these.

"For you? Hook me up with a half, and we'll call it square."

"Half of what?"

"Half pound."

"Mitchell, half pound of what? What the fuck are you talking about?" I answered, starting to get frustrated.

"Man, hook me up with a half-pound of weed! Dude, are you a cop? I didn't think it would be this difficult," Mitchell exclaimed as he shuffled around to the other side of the table.

"Yes! Mitchell, I am a cop! Ya dumb sonofabitch!"

His eyes got wide, and he smiled and then started laughing like only Mitchell can laugh.

He pointed at me with both hands, "Gotcha, muthafucka!"

"Good Lord, you're a tool!"

Once he regained his composure, I asked him again how much for all the items. He replied $200.

"Fine, I'll do two hundred dollars. How much for the vest and jacket?"

"What all ya want on the vest?"

"I need some patches on there. Some that don't say I'm a cop."

"Brother, I got some patches for ya! Check these out."

Mitchell opened a plastic Rubber Maid container and removed numerous small transparent plastic containers with various patches inside. He opened all the containers in a nice neat order and began to pick out patches. He elegantly laid out the patches on a table as if it were fine jewelry.

"Here ya go. This one is 'DILIGAF.' You have to have this on there. You're a vet so this one is good."

He handed me a black patch with red lettering and red boarder "VET."

"Ya need this one, too." He chuckled as he handed me a patch that said "felon" in yellow lettering on a gray background.

Mitchell slid some more patches across the table to me; a Harley Owners group patch, a Sturgis '99 patch, a skeleton hand with the middle finger up, an American flag, and a Confederate flag. Then to top it off, he handed me an "SS" patch. The "SS" patch is the lightning bolts from Hitler's storm troopers in World War II. I gave him a green faded US Marine name tape from my BDU's when I was in the Corps.

"Put this one on, too." I requested.

"I love it! This is goin' to be badass!" Mitchell exclaimed as he snatched up the patches and went to the metal circle clothing rack with all the vests.

"Here, pick one out. You said two XL, right?"

"Yep, two XL."

Mitchell slid the vests one by one on the steel rack until he found the one he liked. He held it up. "This?"

I shook my head.

"How 'bout this one?"

"Nope."

He moved a couple more. I stopped him. I reached to the rack and picked out a distressed black vest with leather laces entwined on the edges. It had bronze snaps and loose leather straps about eight inches hanging from the side seams and two pockets on the lower half of the vest. There were also two inside pockets.

"This one. This is the one." I held it up and inspected it further.

This is badass, I thought to myself.

"How much?" I asked, fearing the answer.

Mitchell could see that I was going to take it regardless of the price, so he highballed me, "Three hundo."

"Really, Mitchell? You can do better than that."

"Fine, two fifty."

"I'll take it."

I gladly accepted, knowing that I would have paid three hundred dollars for it.

"Mitchell, I have some more patches I need you to sew on the vest. But this is some top-secret level shit, you *cannot* say a fuckin' word to anyone, ya understand?"

"Brother, you fall under the attorney-client confidentiality here. I won't say a word," he responded, then pretended to zip his mouth shut and throw the imaginary key over his right shoulder.

I shook my head and smiled. "I'll be right back." And turned to run out to my truck.

I brought in a black and gray backpack and set it on the counter in front of Mitchell. He slid his chair back a couple of feet in anticipation. I reached in and retrieved a lower rocker patch that said "Iowa" in black lettering on a light gray background with black bordering. The next one was a three-inch by three-inch patch with "MC." Next was a two-inch by two-inch patch with the number "13," then the top rocker "Pale Riders." And finally, the center patch, a larger circle with the Grim Reaper riding a white horse wielding a big ass medieval hammer. The horse was jumping through red flames. And the saying scrolled on the top into the bottom of the patch said, "Behold I saw a Pale Horse, it's rider named death and hell followed."

Mitchell's eyes were as big as baseballs by this point.

"What the fuck is this? Where did ya get this? Who da fuck are the Pale Riders MC?" he asked without taking a breath.

"I told you, this is some next level shit right here. You can't say a word to anyone. If you do, I will be killed." I reasoned, maybe a little over the top, but understand who I was talking to.

"We're good, man." Mitchell started inspecting all the patches and placing them in order on the vest to see how it will look and just as suspected…Badass!

"I made this club up. It does not exist, yet. I had an embroidery guy make these, and then I destroyed the blueprint. We are the only ones that know about this. I will be wearing this when I buy contraband. So, if you see me at a rally or swap meet, you gotta be cool."

I reached into my pocket of my jeans and pulled out two more patches. I handed them to Mitchell like I was handing him a gold brick. He held out his hands and smiled from ear to ear.

"Perfect!" was his only response.

The patches were three inches by one inch each. One said, "Sergeant at Arms" and the other "Preacher." This is how all the people that I buy dope from will know me as from now on...Preacher.

"Ya know where these go, right?" I asked in confidence.

"Oh ya!" is all he said.

Mitchell gained his composure and asked, "When do you want these done?"

"Now, Mitchell, I need them now."

"That's what I thought. Let's do this! There's beer in the fridge." He pointed to the small brown dorm room refrigerator in the corner of the sewing room.

I popped open a can of Budweiser and made myself comfortable on the tweed and wood 1970s style couch. Lynyrd Skynyrd came on the stereo as if on cue.

Three hours, ten cigarettes, and six beers later, Mitchell was finished. He brushed off the vest and folded in the front, so it looks proper for the inspection. Without saying a word, he motioned for me to come over to his sewing area and see his masterpiece. He sat on his sewing stool and wiped the sweat from his forehead.

I gazed at the vest as if it were a Rembrandt or Picasso; in this case, it was. The rarest outlaw motorcycle club colors in the world. The patches were set specifically in their final resting place to signify the résumé of a Sergeant of Arms outlaw biker.

I turned the vest over to inspect the back. I held it up and smiled. A lone tear rolled down my face as I read and reread the saying, "Behold I saw a Pale Horse, it's rider named death and hell followed."

I glanced at Mitchell. "I love it."

"Me, too, this is the coolest thing I have ever made, I swear to God! Now put it on!"

I slid my left arm through the armhole, then my right arm and adjusted the vest as if it were my newly knitted body armor. I felt ten feet tall and bulletproof.

"Fuck, dude, if I saw you riding your bike with that on, I would not fuck with you."

That's exactly what I was thinking!

A biker's colors are one of the most important items to them. The order of importance is, colors, motorcycle, woman, and then dog. The colors are usually a three-piece set with the top rocker the name of the club. The bottom rocker is the location of the club, usually state or city or if they are from nowhere, it will say "nomad." The center patch will be the insignia that identifies the club. Probably the most popular set of colors is the Hell's Angels' death head. Typically, another patch seen on the front and the back of the colors is the "1%" insignia. This is usually inside a diamond or a circle, although I have seen just the "1%" as a patch and not encompassed in a shape. The "1%" stands for the outlaw biker creed or persona—the badass, the rebel, or the outlaw.

The one percenter originated in Hollister, California, during the bike rally in 1947. After nights of drunken bar fights with the outlaw bikers, a representative from the AMA (American Motorcycle Association) said, "Ninety-nine percent of motorcyclists are good, decent, law-abiding citizens."

This was taken as the other "1 percent" were not good, decent, and law-abiding citizens, hence the name "1%er."

Many outlaw motorcycle clubs have this moniker somewhere on their cuts and also tattooed on their body. Even engraved or painted on their bikes. They wear rings, necklaces, belt buckles, and "soft colors." Soft colors are T-shirts or sweatshirts that have the club's moniker and/or symbols on them. These are generally worn by actual members and not the public. However, the public can purchase club accessories on their website or at bike rallies.

I knew a member of a club who had a ring made with a backward "1%" in a diamond so that when he punched someone in the forehead, the guy would see it the right way in the mirror.

I have seen "1%er" tattoos on hands, necks, arms, chest, shoulders, and backs. There are several bylaws with each different club on how a club member can get a "1%er" tattoo. It will differ for each club. This does not mean that a club not showing the "1%er" patch is not affiliated with a larger outlaw club. One does not learn about outlaw bikers by reading, it is on the job training. Here, endeth the lesson.

After long deliberation, decided to not attach a "1%er" patch to my colors. Why? Typically, an unknown club not affiliated with a larger club cannot have the patch on their cuts. This will cause a lot of problems for me if I run into a larger group that uses the "1%er" patch. I do have a silver and black ring that I will use when I buy dope, as long as I'm not buying dope from an outlaw biker, I should be okay. It might help me, actually, as you will see later, it will help me.

CHAPTER 13

Timmy and I met at our usual rendezvous spot, the cemetery. This time, it was about midafternoon on a Friday. We needed to go to Hastings to meet with the sheriff's deputy narcotic officer and his partner. He had some information regarding some local dopers and wanted us to try and buy some meth from them. Apparently, they have been trying to bust these guys for quite a while and were unsuccessful.

I waited in my POS truck for Timmy because he's special and is on his own time—"doper's time." As I sat there in the cemetery, I mentally went over various scenarios of things that have not happened or could possibly happen and won't ever happen. It's a way I psychologically prepare myself for undercover operations. There's not a lot of thought that goes into acting like a doper; unless you aren't a doper, then it becomes difficult.

As I sat there contemplating, I lit a cigarette and took a big inhale and released the smoke. I muffled a cough as I just started smoking again after a few years of not smoking. I'm still trying to acclimate my lungs. I used my Zippo lighter that I received from a bunch of my Marine buddies when I was discharged from the Corps. It has a special engraving on it of my unit, 3/3 Kilo Co. On the other side, it says "Preacher." Preacher was my childhood nickname and carried over to the Corps when I was a radio operator for my platoon.

I see Timmy peddling his little legs off on "his" BMX bike riding toward me down the white rock road of the cemetery. I sat waiting, smiling at the site that I'm witnessing. A wheelie here, a bunny hop there, then a powerslide in front of the truck.

"Get in!" I yelled at Timmy. Not a "Hi, how are you?" or "What's up?" just a "get in."

"Timmy, we got to go to Hastings today. Do you know anything new?" I asked as Timmy got in and settled into the seat.

"Nope, nothing."

"Are you sure? Think."

"Well."

There it is, this kid, I tell you. It's like pulling teeth from a tweaker, I thought to myself.

"So, I may have some information for you about a dude here in town."

"Go on."

"His name is Chris and works at West Star Company."

"Does Chris have a last name?"

"Ya, Swanson."

"Swanson? Chris Swanson? Is he about twenty-five, fat, blonde hair, and drives a blue piece of shit Pontiac Grand Prix?" I questioned, now very curious.

"Ya, how tha fuck you know that?" Timmy turned to me with amazement.

"I went to high school with his sister. He became a doper and then moved to this area."

I put the truck in gear and drove through the cemetery toward the county road and turned north to go visit the "metropolis" of Hastings.

"Tell me more about what you know with Chris."

"So, Chris works at West Star and has been there for about two years. He has a supplier from some small town that uses him to deliver meth to factory workers."

"Go on."

"So, he gets his shipment on Thursdays and hands it out to the workers, and they pay him on Fridays, which is payday."

"So, he fronts them the dope and then gets paid on Friday?"

"Yep," Timmy responded arrogantly like he knew something no one else did.

Hmmm... That's smart. There is no money exchanged at the time so if he does get caught on Thursday, only the drugs will get seized and on Fridays, only the money would get seized, I thought to myself.

"Tell me more, do you know the people he's selling to? Do you know his supplier?"

"Well, I know his supplier is an Asian stripper or hooker, or both."

I lit another cigarette; this is not good that I'm smoking like this again. I'll quit after the operation.

"Timmy, I can't buy from Chris. He knows who I am. So, if we were to work him, you'd have to buy from him. Will he sell to you?" I asked, puffing on my rekindled bad habit.

"Ya, sure."

"Have you bought from him before?"

There was a long pause and Timmy stared straight forward, not looking at me. I slapped his arm with a back hand and asked again.

"Have you bought from him before?"

"Ya," he said, looking down and fidgeting with his hands.

"He's your supplier, isn't he?"

"Ya." Timmy, still in the same position.

Timmy continued with information regarding Chris and this Asian stripper. I would bet ten to one that she is not a stripper. Chris went to high school with her, and she gets her supply from California. She has anywhere from an ounce to pounds of quality meth, not this "Annie Cook" meth from Iowa.

It's called "Annie Cook" meth because of one of the main ingredients in the cooking of the meth is anhydrous ammonia. This method is also called the "Nazi Cook," due to the Nazi soldiers given meth during World War II in order to fight better and longer. The anhydrous ammonia is a primary ingredient to extract the pseudoephedrine from the tablets, which, after about a two-hour process, makes the final product of methamphetamine.

Chris lives in our little town, but the Asian stripper, Joy, lives in Hastings, which is also in a different county. I explained to Timmy that we need to start getting the drugs out of our community. I am starting to think Timmy does not want that and keeps giving me people from elsewhere. However, Chris would be a good one to get but will be more challenging as I won't be buying the dope from him. Timmy will be.

As we arrived at the sheriff's office, I reminded Timmy to keep his mouth shut unless asked a direct question. These guys do not mess around and are not big fans of people like Timmy. Timmy agreed.

I buzzed the door waiting for approval to enter the building. Once inside, we were met with my handler, Russell. We shook hands and were escorted to the offices. Sitting at the conference table were the other narcotics deputy and two guys I did not know. They stood up and introduced themselves as Special Agent Thompson and Special Agent Lyons of the Department of Narcotics Enforcement (DNE).

"These gentlemen have heard how well you are doing with your CI and want to assist us," Russell explained with apprehension.

"Hmmm."

Timmy was staring at me. I glared at him, and he put his head down and looked at the floor.

"Russ, can I speak to you? Out here?" I requested to Russell as I pointed outside the conference room.

"Sure. Gentlemen, we'll be right back. Make yourselves at home," Russell stated politician-like to the agents.

"Timmy, sit. Don't say a word."

"Mmkay."

We stepped out of the conference room. I waited until Russell was clear from the door and shut it gently.

"What the fuck, Russ!"

"These guys are interested in helping with the operation. That's all."

"Bullshit, they want to take the glory and show everyone how great of a job they did and all the bad guys they got off the street. They're going to want me to introduce them to our targets, then they're going to cut us out and tell us they have it from here and will call us if they need help. Then when they do the busts, they have you standing perimeter while their teams take down all the bad guys. And you know this is how it's going to go." All in one breath, I explained to Russell emphatically, all the while, he nodded his head in an understanding way.

"This isn't your decision," Russell rebutted.

"Whoa! We wouldn't be having this conversation without me and you know that. I'm the one that can get in with these guys."

Russell interrupted me. "You haven't got in with them yet."

"Yes, but my CI will get me in, and he's my CI." I emphasized "my."

Russell put his hand on my left shoulder. "Look, let's just hear what they have to say and go from there."

"Fine, but if I don't like it, we walk."

"Agreed."

We reentered the conference room. Russell walked around to the opposite side of the table, and I sat next to Timmy. Man, he needs to shower more. The two agents had fancy black leather legal-size notebooks and pads of paper out in front of them, pens in hand ready to rewrite their narrative.

Agent Thompson spoke first. "It sounds like you guys know quite a bit information regarding the twins."

Timmy nodded in agreeance. I nudged him and said, "I wouldn't say quite a bit."

"Can you tell us what you know?" Agent Thompson asked.

"Not yet, I don't have all the information. Once I get it, then I'll get it to you."

"Look, we're on your side, we just want to help," Agent Thompson replied as he sat back in his chair and leaned back to the limit of the recliner.

"If you're on our side, then you'll have patience and wait until I can get all the intel. I'll get it to you then."

Agent Thompson stood up and stepped back from the table. He reached over the chair and folded his note-book shut, inserted his pen into the interior pocket of his government-issued blazer, and tapped his partner on his shoulder. Agent Lyons took two business cards with all the contact information except their cell phone numbers out of his folder and placed them on the table; didn't hand them to me, just set them on the table. Real personable, this guy. They walked out of the conference room and out of sight. I heard the security door buzz, open, and then close with a thud and click.

"That was fun," I cynically stated under my breath.

"Can you introduce Phil to the twins?" Russell asked in an authoritative way to Timmy.

Timmy looked at me as if to say, *Can I answer?* I nodded.

"Yep, no problem," Timmy said with a smile.

"Let's get this started then," Russell said confidently.

139

CHAPTER 14

After the debriefing with Russell and his partner forwarding him all the information, we made arrangements to start surveillance on the area. This will aid us in conducting a safe operation. We will start the drug buys within the next week or two. In the meantime, Timmy and I are going to start the intel process on Chris and try and get three buys once the operation in Hastings is complete.

Russell escorted us to the back door and wished us well. We hopped into the old Ford pickup and backed out of the parking lot of the sheriff's office. Once we pulled out to the street, we passed two local police squad cars. I did the friendly Midwest one finger wave from the top of the steering wheel. They did not wave back.

I looked in the rearview mirror and watched the officers make a U-turn in the parking lot and exit where they entered. They proceeded to follow us. I didn't know at the time if they were following us or if they were just going the same direction. I saw a Kum & Go convenient store a couple of blocks ahead and decided to stop there and get an energy drink.

As I pulled into the parking stall in front of the store, I watched the cruisers enter the parking lot as well. One pulled in behind me at an angle, and the other came to a stop on the passenger side of my truck. Both officers exited their vehicles at the same time. Prior to the stop, I'm sure they ran my plates. I have government-issued license plates that, when checked by law enforcement, come back as "not on file." This means the plates can go on any vehicle and are usually on vehicles driven by law enforcement. But sometimes, it means the plates are possibly illegal. The officers were hoping it was the latter.

I looked to my right and saw the officer with his right hand on his sidearm and the strap unsnapped as he walked toward my truck. This is common on traffic stops. Anyone who experiences this may feel it is intimidating. Even for me, I was a little uneasy, especially when the officer who parked behind us opened my door and told me to get out.

I complied and stepped out slowly. He stood there blocking my exit, so I had to slide by him closer than I liked. You know, when you're in a bar and someone slams their shoulder into yours trying to be a tough guy, that was this officer's power move, just a sign of intimidation. Did it work? Nope.

The other officer told Timmy to get out of the truck and step to the rear between the squad car and the pickup. By this time, people were starting to mill around the front of the store. This was before everyone had a smartphone with a camera, but I know there will be video from the security camera, if it's working.

As I was walking to the rear of the pickup, apparently, I wasn't walking fast enough because the officer pushed me from behind without warning. I took a couple steps forward, regained my balance, and turned to him.

"So, you're that cop," I said under my breath, emphasizing "that."

"Whatcha say to me, boy?" he responded.

I arrived at the back, and Timmy was watching me to see how I would handle the shakedown that the two local cops were giving us.

"Fellas, you're making a mistake here. I don't know what you think we did, but if you let me explain, I think we can go about our evenings without further interaction." I bargained in my most politically correct tone.

"Shut up. Give me your license," was the officer's response.

I reached for my wallet on the chain and unsnapped the leather flap covering the wallet. Inside my wallet, I have a zipped compartment with my fake Iowa driver's license, a fake insurance card for my truck, a fake credit card that doesn't work, bail bonds business cards, an attorney's business card, some tattoo cards, and random names and numbers on a piece of paper. This is considered by law enforcement to be "wallet trash."

Remember, this was before smartphones when we had to keep all the information from a phone in our wallets. Nothing in my wallet will give my real identity to the officers. I didn't know who these guys were, and I didn't want them to know who I was, yet. Also, with all the lookie-loos watching, I didn't want my cover blown. I've had that happen, and it's not a pleasant experience.

I handed the officer my driver's license by holding it with my hand not fully extended and keeping it waist high. This is a doper's power move, making the officer extend his arm to retrieve the ID. The officer knew what I was doing and mumbled something about my hygiene under his breath. As an undercover operative, I know the dopers' moves and also law enforcement's moves. Was I messing with him? Absolutely.

"Phil Quick? Are you quick?" The officer asked jokingly emphasizing "quick."

I glared at him, trying not to make any facial expressions to let him know he is getting to me.

"What brings you from Muscatine to here? Are you buying dope or selling it?" the officer interrogated me.

My Iowa driver's license shows that I live in Muscatine. My date of birth is the same, minus two years, and my address is the same where I live but different city. The key to an undercover persona is to keep it very similar to real life so you don't have to remember small things in high-stress situations, like when a tweaker has a gun pointed at your head. I'll get to that later.

He continued with the field interview. "When was the last time you used any street drugs, meth, marijuana, cocaine, heroin, PCP, or LSD?"

"I don't use drugs, sir," I responded.

"So, when was the last time you used?" he asked again.

This is an interview tactic taught to street officers. Instead of asking, "Do you use drugs?" the officer will ask, "When was the last time you used?" which implies he or she already knows you use and wants to have confirmation. Since I know the game, "I won't fall for the banana in the tailpipe" (in my best Eddie Murphy impression).

"Look, Officer, I don't use drugs, I don't sell drugs, and I don't have drugs. I have twenty bucks in my wallet. We're trying to find work up here because it's close to the lakes. That's it," I explained.

"Well, Mr. Quick, I have all your information, and if I find you and Timothy here in town again, we're going to have a different conversation. Understand?" The friendly officer leaned in to tell me in a quiet authoritative voice.

I smirked because he called Timmy, "Timothy." I reached my hand out to retrieve my ID. He handed it to me and then gave Timmy his ID. He motioned to the other officer to leave. They returned to their squad cars and left the parking lot. I turned around toward the store and realized why they didn't go further with the inquisition; we gained a rather large audience in front of the store.

Internally, I smiled and would remind myself to write their information down for a later time. Good thing, they didn't search the truck because they would have found my Glock and extra magazines that I slid under the seat when I saw them pull up behind me.

CHAPTER 15

The next three months will be the largest undercover operation that I will have ever conducted. It will include numerous law enforcement agencies throughout the state of Iowa. It will consist of many drug and gun buys with thousands of dollars seized along with pounds of methamphetamine, cocaine, and marijuana. The one thing that I wanted to do in the law enforcement world is to be a deep undercover operative. This case will be a test of wits and stretch the stress limitations of my inner self. After this, everything else is minimal.

When I initially arrested Timmy, the thought of an investigation transpiring to the magnitude of this one was incomprehensible. I believed he would be able to produce some low-level drug dealers who will then roll on their dealer and nothing more. I would then continue with my patrol duties of a uniformed police officer. Man, was I wrong.

Timmy and I met at our usual location in the cemetery on a hot July afternoon. The heat index was 105 degrees and no wind. I normally don't mind the heat when I'm able to dress for it, but wearing blue jeans, biker boots, and a black leather vest will make one cranky in this heat.

Timmy was his normal jovial self. I kind of feel bad for him. He has been dealt a difficult hand of cards. He's not the brightest bulb in the chandelier, but he has potential. Hell, maybe he's growing on me.

The sheriff's office in Hastings had been collecting intelligence on the twins for the last week, surveilling the residence and documenting all the comings and goings of potential targets of opportunity. When Timmy and I arrived at the SO, we met with Russell, my handler. Russell will oversee the entire operation from here on out.

Russell has been the chief deputy for about five years, but he's been a deputy sheriff for twenty years. Russell is about six feet, one inch and a beer gut who hangs over his black leather duty belt when in uniform.

The sheriff has assigned him to my case agent solely, so he's not overdoing it and getting burned out. Russell has neatly trimmed tight haircut with salt and pepper coloring. A light gray goatee to accentuate his piercing wise blue eyes. Russell is old school; where many law enforcement officers carry Glocks, Berettas, or Sig Sauers, he carries a Colt 1911 Gold Cup with three extra seven-round magazines. The black engraving on the silver slide indicated his US Army unit he served with before becoming a deputy.

Russell has a very sarcastic sense of humor bordering on racist. But if you've seen the things that he has in his career, you would feel the same way. He is a hot rod fanatic and even drives a matte black 1923 T-Bucket Roadster on the weekends to car shows in the area. He has spent a lot of time and money on that car. Above all else, Russell is a hard worker and an honest man.

We exchanged pleasantries when we arrived and made sure all was good with each other. He escorted us to the conference room where three other law enforcement officers were waiting. They were conversing among each other, drinking energy drinks and bottles of water.

I knew one of the deputies, Brandon Pearson. He's been a deputy for about ten years and a guy you want on your side in a fight. He's not a huge towering force, but what he lacks in size, he makes up in heart. He's wiry and mean when it comes to fighting. I called him sneaky strong; he didn't look like much then. *Bam!* You're on your back, breathing snot bubbles trying to collect yourself.

The other two deputies, I did not know directly. I've heard of them from being on the tactical team but didn't know much about them. One is Jason, a six-foot, four-inch towering White man with a lot of tats on his arms that are about the size of tree trunks. I would stand behind him in a firefight.

The other deputy is Nick, the only Black law enforcement officer in the area. When people can't remember his name, they say, "You know, the Black one." So as a joke, we all call him the "Black One." To a normal person outside of law enforcement, this would not be funny, but to us and him, it is. Nick is about five feet, ten inches and has a shave head. He is built like a brick shit house, is a former fullback in college and sustained a lot, and I mean a lot of concussions. He can bench press over four hundred pounds and squat six-fifty. But his favorite number is orange. Another real good guy to have on our side.

I stood behind a high back black leather office chair tapping my fingers in tempo while looking at each deputy and appreciating their acceptance of this job. This will not be easy. It will be hard testing the limits of their testicular fortitude. Fun, it will be fun!

"Gentlemen, thank you for meeting with us and accepting this duty assignment. We are going to have fun, but also, it will be very challenging. I am putting my life in your hands. Timmy's life in your hands. Are you willing to take on this responsibility?" I asked with a serious, stern tone.

The four deputies looked at each other and then at me and in unison, busted out laughing and pointing.

"You sound like such a tool!"

"Dude, really?"

"Ha, ha, very funny, you assholes!" I rebutted as I sat down in the chair I was standing behind.

Timmy looked around scared and confused. I began to laugh and realize how stupid I sounded. There were document folders in front of all of us. A lot of the information was new to me as I had not been part of the surveillance part of the operation. The folders were nicely done and in order, not like the makeshift files we usually see. Brandon stood up and walked to a dry erase board covered by a white roll-up screen like what you would see in a classroom. He released the tension of the screen and guided it up to the top. On the board were photos of people, vehicles, houses, mobile homes, and RVs.

"Here are the future residents of our fine jail facility. Fellas, the pictures in the middle are the 'twins.' They are our primaries." Brandon pointed out on the board.

"All their information is in the packet in front of you. Sorry, dude, you don't get one," he said to Timmy.

Timmy smiled and looked down.

I explained to Timmy there will be some things we will discuss in here that he will not be privy to, and he'll have to step out of the room.

Brandon went on with the intel.

"Mikey and Jeremy are twenty-five-year-old twins who live with their mom and stepdad. They made the garage into an apartment for the twins while Mom and Pop live in the trailer. The trailer is in Wolf Park, a mile north of town. There are two ways in and out and it sits in a horseshoe configuration."

He continued.

"The twins sell meth, weed, and coke. They are known to have and carry guns. And they are always tweaking. There is a party there every weekend from Friday to Sunday. The neighbors are fed up with them and want us to do whatever it takes to get them out of there."

"Phil, you and Timmy will be buying as much shit as you can get. They are not cooking the meth, and we don't know who is bringing in the coke and weed. That is what you need to find out. What do you think?"

I looked at the file, then up to the board and smiled.

"Hell, ya I can do that."

For the next hour, I had Timmy sit outside while we went over confidential information regarding the case. He got to sit with Linda, a sweet older lady who loves to talk baseball and knew more about it than I ever will.

We covered all communications, avenues of approach and escape, emergency signals, weapons, buy money, cover locations, etc. These are things someone like Timmy does not need to know.

Once the meeting was over, Jason and Nick left to set up cover in the area of the trailer park. They will be there for two hours before the green light is given for my entrance. I will never know their exact location. Brandon will be following Timmy and I in his UC car, a gray 1995 Ford Thunderbird. He will follow to make sure no one comes up from behind and is also in direct communication with me.

Russell's position is overseeing the operation and making sure it runs smoothly for the buys and logging in all the evidence. This is very important in an operation of this magnitude because of the amount of people and money. Good support is always welcome and needed.

After two hours of chilling at the SO, Timmy and I drove to the mobile home park in my undercover shit brown 1976 Ford F100 pickup. With Brandon close behind, we made our way through town and out to the main highway that will take us to Wolf Park.

Wolf Park has been a local mobile home park for about forty years. It used to be respectable but has become more of an eyesore and habitat for low income or no income families. Once the drive-in movie theater shut down in 1991, it became really rundown. The manager is an onsite manager but is only responsible for retrieving rent from the tenants. He is supposed to help with general maintenance but is too fat and lazy to do much more than walk to his refrigerator.

The yards, if you can call them that, are primarily dirt with broken-down vehicles and other machinery, old children's toys, and a picnic table here and there. Boarded-up windows and tilted mobile homes finish off the "ghetto" as the locals call it.

Jeremy and Mikey live in a renovated white trailer with a two-car detached garage that was transformed into an apartment for them. The mother and stepfather live in the trailer with a female cousin. The trailer is a typical configuration with the front door opening to the living room and kitchen area. There are three bedrooms in the back with a bathroom between the two smaller bedrooms. The master bedroom is at the back of the trailer. There is new carpet and fresh interior paint. The windows are higher quality than a normal trailer to help with the cold Iowa winters. New electrical and plumbing throughout the mobile home round out the renovations. This was all paid for by drug money from Jeremy and Mikey.

The garage sits about forty feet from the trailer with a car port between the two. The garage car door was removed and replaced with a wall. The walk-in door has a storm door and exterior door. A bathroom was installed in the corner of the garage with a shower, toilet, and sink. A small walk-in closet was built next to the bathroom.

On the opposite side of the bathroom, a kitchenette like seen in an extended stay hotel was installed. The boys have two full-size beds along the north wall and a fifty-inch flat screen television on the opposite wall. Posters of scantily clad women, beer, and Harleys were littered upon the walls as their motif.

The makeshift apartment was relatively clean aside from the stale odor of beer, liquor, and smoke. For young dopers, the place was clean, due to the fact they had women come over and clean for drugs. I guess they could be doing other things instead.

This location is well known for extended parties. Jeremy and Mikey do not have gainful employment other than selling their product to the locals. It is well known that if one needs just about any kind of drug, they can come here and get it. Meth, coke, weed, prescription pills, shrooms, and ecstasy. They do not sell heroin, LSD or PCP. I guess they have some morals...

They were rumored to be selling firearms, ammunition, and body armor. This had not been confirmed at this point but hopefully will soon.

Their stepdad James or "Jimmy" is a patch holder for the Sons of Violence MC and is a silent partner of the twin's enterprise. Jimmy's trailer is a temporary clubhouse for the SOVMC North Iowa chapter. Jimmy has been a member for about twenty or so years but does not hold a rank in the chapter. There are about fifteen patch holders and five prospects and countless hang arounds in Jimmy's chapter.

The prospect, a person who is trying to gain the trust of the chapter members to become a member. This process typically takes anywhere from six months to a year. Sometimes longer. Prospects are usually the ones who have something to prove to the club and are willing to do what it takes to get into the club.

This means committing crimes, working endless hours, or catering to the needs of the club. Providing security, washing the bikes, serving drinks, cooking food, and starting fights. At a law enforcement standpoint, these guys are the ones who are carrying illegal guns and drugs. It's not as big of a deal for a prospect to get busted than it is a member.

Hang arounds are guys trying to get to the status of prospect and really have nothing to do with the club's business. They go to their parties, runs (extended rides), swap meets, funerals, weddings, etc. Sometimes, the hang arounds do not want to be in the club and conduct club business. They just want to hang with the club.

The members or patch holders are the only ones who can conduct club business. They usually follow a militaristic guideline for rank and structure. For example, the president of the club is the highest rank. The president of the club and the president of the chapter are different in rank and file. However, they can be both. Then there are the vice presidents, the sergeant at arms, captains, lieutenants, road captains, secretary and treasury, drug dealers, mechanics, gun runners, and so on.

A captain and road captain are different ranks. The road captain is the one in charge of the route taken from place to place. They have a strong knowledge of the highways, law enforcement gas stations, locations of rival gangs, and back roads. A captain is a leadership rank like a lieutenant.

The sergeant at arms is the security for the club. Another name for them is the enforcer. Each club have different names for the respective positions. The sergeant at arms is the one who sets up the security and does all the investigations for the chapters.

For example, the background checks for prospects, information on local law enforcement, security at events, runs, and rallies. They are also the ones in charge of "in-house" issues between members and help establish bylaws and rules in the club. These are typically the baddest, most violent experience, or military background, but not always.

The vice president is the president's right-hand man. They will take over in the absence of the president. They are the ones who oversee the other ranks as well.

Unfortunately, law enforcement has not been proactive when it comes to outlaw bikers. There have been some instances of large investigations but not a lot. The RICO case in 1994 in Iowa and a few in California and Florida that were well known, but at that time not a lot. There had since been intelligence organizations and task forces put into place by the government after they realized that the outlaw bikers transport a lot of contraband and pose a real threat to the American public.

CHAPTER 16

Timmy and I entered the mobile home park, Wolf Park, and proceeded down the dusty gravel road riddled with potholes and cracks. The bent-over "10 mph" sign at the entrance was more of a suggestion than a law. It seems we have entered into lawlessness. My police eyes scanned the area looking for a threat. I felt that I have two brains—one for law enforcement and the other for crime. I cross over at an instance and at any given time, my left arm resting on the window opening of the door as I casually sit in the beat-up truck. I felt my mouth became dry and my blood pressure elevated.

We followed the road to Jeremy and Mikey's trailer and parked in front of the garage. Timmy has now become nervous and fidgety.

"You ready for this?" I asked Timmy, not really expecting an answer.

He nodded in agreeance.

"Who am I?" I asked.

"My cousin Preacher from Des Moines," he stammered.

"Good. Let's do this."

We exited the pickup and walked across the gravel driveway to the front door of the garage. The curtain on the kitchen window of the trailer closed as I caught a glimpse of a silhouette. Timmy knocked on the door, not a super-secret knock, just a knock. I stood behind him and to the side in a tactical position for me, but someone watching wouldn't even think about it.

The heavy exterior door opened. There stood Mikey with blue gym shorts, Nike sliders, and no shirt. Random homemade tats riddled his chest and arms. A few scars from fights and drunk nights of showing off. He gave a spry smile and stood behind the storm door with the screen opened.

"Hello, Tim! How are you?" he asked in a polite manner, which I was not expecting.

"I'm doing well, Mikey, thanks for asking," he replied.

I lowered my sunglasses to get an unbiased view of what I was seeing and hearing. What the hell is this?

"Whose yer friend, Tim?"

"Umm, he's not my friend, he's my cousin from Des Moines."

"Does yer cousin have a name, or should I call him 'cousin from Des Moines'?"

"Ya, ya. No, it's Preacher. His name is Preacher."

I reached my hand out to shake his hand and properly introduced myself, "Preacher."

Mikey opened the storm door and stepped outside. The door eased itself closed behind him.

"Well, hello, Preacher, Tim's cousin from Des Moines," he said as he grasped my hand in the weakest grip I have ever felt.

It really made me feel uneasy.

"What brings you here today for, Tim?"

"We would like some white, if you have any."

Mikey's eyes unlocked with me, and his head whipped to the side to stare down Timmy.

"Not out here," he said as he turned and opened the door and entered the garage.

The door closed before I could reach the handle. I reopened it and followed Mikey; Timmy close behind. The garage was tidy and organized. The TV was on and there on the only couch sat Jeremy who instantly stood up.

Well, shit…

I knew someday I would run into this guy again. Today is the day. I had to control this situation before it got out of hand.

"Hey, I know you!" I said quickly before he could get a word out.

Mikey spun around and stared at me, then to Jeremy.

"What's he talkin' about?"

"Ya, I met Jeremy at Glenn's one night. 'Member? This muthafucka thought I was a cop. I'm starting to think maybe you tha cop." I mitigated the situation.

"What!? Oh bullshit, dude! I ain't no cop!" Jeremy countered.

And then I heard the unforgettable and completely recognizable sound of the pump action of a twelve-gauge shotgun. I turned and found myself looking at the business end of a shotty. Mikey had retrieved his sawed-off shotgun from the bedframe and was about to open my skull like a watermelon.

"You betta start talkin' muthafucka!" Mikey emphatically said while removing the safety switch of the Mossberg.

"Hey, what the fuck are we doing?" I looked at Timmy, who is trying not to piss himself.

"J, where do you know this fool from?" Mikey asked.

"I met this dude at Glenn's before he got busted. It was one night when Sarah and I needed some shit. Him and his buddy showed up outta tha blue."

I could see the hamster start running to spin the wheel in Mikey's head. He began to lower the shotgun to my midsection when I decided to make my move. I knew in my head this was going to go one of two ways; either he was going to pull the trigger, or he would put the gun down. But I had to do something, and this was my best option, or was it.

As soon as he looked to Jeremy, I reached behind my back and pulled my Glock in one swift motion with my right hand and pointed it at his face. I explained to him in a calm, even-keel tone that if he pulls the trigger, the reaction would be my finger depressing the five-and-a-half-pound trigger to release the lead bullet into his forehead. His reaction...he lowered the shotgun.

Internally, I was breathing a sigh of relief and clinching my bladder, so I don't piss myself in front of everyone. On the outside, "I was as cool as the other side of the pillow," to quote the great Stuart Scott.

"Enough of this nonsense," Mikey said without emotion.

"What is it that you need on this beautiful day, Timmy?" he continued.

"Well, Preacher, here, is a member of a motorcycle club, and they're having a big ass party this weekend. So we lookin' to score for his club. Then maybe continue the relationship. Ya know what I mean?" Timmy explained while trying not to stare at the illegal shotgun still in Mikey's hand.

"I see. This sounds like something I can work with. First things first. And I do apologize, this is only business, but I do have to ask…"

Mikey stepped close to me and broke the comfort of my personal barrier and put his nose within one inch of mine and stared into my eyes with cold, hollow blue eyes.

"I will sell to you. But… If I find out you are a cop, I *will* kill you and your entire family. Is there any doubt in your mind, right now, that I am not serious?"

I shook my head to indicate no and said, "I'm not a cop, you don't have to worry, and you will make a lot of cash."

"Fantastic!" Mikey slapped his left hand down onto my shoulder, both of us still grasping onto our firearms. "Let's do this!"

"J, retrieve the product for our new friend, please," Mikey asked Jeremy in his polite tone.

Jeremy stood up from the couch and walked out of the garage. A short time later, he returned with a blue generic duffle bag. He set it on the bed and unzipped the bag and opened it. He pulled out two clear bags with white crystal-line powder and five with green leafy substance. Each bag was one pound. Apparently, they only deal with pounds and not kilos. It does not really matter to me how they package it. It's just more evidence that needs to be logged in.

"How much?" I asked.

"Twenty for the white and five for the green," Mikey responded.

I stroked my goatee pretending to be thinking. Timmy sat down on the corner of the bed like his legs gave out. He began to rub his temples.

"Done," I said in agreement.

"Fantastic!" Mikey clapped his hands together, then held open his hands to receive the money. "How 'bout it?"

"I have one grand on me and need to make a call to get the rest. Can I give ya the one and bring the rest tonight?" I asked, hoping he was a reasonable businessman.

"So, you want it all, but don't have the money on you, is that what I'm hearing?" he asked.

"I wasn't going to bring twenty K to a guy I've never met, then you shoot me and take my club's money. That's not smart business, brah."

He interrupted me, "Twenty-five."

"Ya, fifty-five K."

"All I have to do is make a call, and I can bring you the rest. That simple. I mean, if you don't want it."

"When can you have it here?"

I looked at my watch, 2015 hours. I explained to him that I can meet my guy at 9:00 p.m., then be back here before ten. Mikey contemplated and looked at Jeremy, who gave his typical response by shrugging his shoulders. Mikey rolled his eyes and then turned back to me.

"Ten p.m.?"

"Yep."

"Leave the grand for good faith money, and I'll see you at ten. Any surprises and yer dead, got it?"

I nodded and signaled for Timmy to exit the garage. We hopped into the pickup and followed the gravel road to the blacktop. I checked the rearview mirror and side mirrors to see if anyone was following. Nothing. I waited for the car to pass by us and entered the roadway. The relief feeling rushed through me, and I'm not sure why since it was not over. Actually, the only thing I did was leave a thousand dollars with a doper in the hopes that I can get the rest of it later.

We arrived at the sheriff's office and met with Brandon and Russ.

"How did it go?" Russ asked.

"Well, the good news is, they believed that I am a biker and need a lot of shit. The bad news is, I need another twenty-four thousand dollars."

Russ reached for the stair railing and sat down on the steps, trying to collect himself.

"Twenty-four thousand? Seriously? For what?"

"One key of crystal meth and five pounds of high-grade weed."

"Oh, is that all?"

I chuckled. "Yep, that's all."

"How many buys do you think you can get from these guys?"

"As many as we want. These guys want money, and if we keep producing money, they'll keep selling."

"Fine, I can get that. When do you need it by?"

I started laughing, Brandon began laughing, and then Timmy started laughing, not knowing why we were laughing.

"Ten."

"What tha fuck, Phil? Are you serious? I can't get it by ten o'clock!"

"Well, ya kinda have to. Otherwise, I'm dead."

"Fuck!" Russ said in a stifled huff.

There are not a lot of law enforcement agencies that have twenty-four thousand dollars on hand at any given time. This is not something that they do. Large departments have that money though. Russ made a phone call to a friend at a department who owed him a favor. The department was a larger one that has that kind of money in evidence. However, to save time, we needed another favor—they need to bring it to us at a very high rate of speed. I'm sure they can find a rookie who is willing to transport twenty-four K in a marked squad car at a hundred miles an hour. This is the only way we can get it in time.

At nine forty, the officer arrived and pulled into the garage. We took photos of all the money and filled out the receipt for the officer to take back to his department. I threw it in a brand-new duffle bag and tossed it in my pickup.

"Let's go, Timmy!"

We backed the truck out of the sally port and sped off to the mobile home park with Brandon hot on our heels. He contacted Nick and Jason and explained what was going on and asked if there was anything new at the trailer. All was quiet, and the time is now 9:55 p.m.

I fishtailed into the gravel drive of the mobile home park and slowed down to gain control. The truck made a complete stop in front of Mikey and Jeremy's trailer. I regained my composure and took a couple of big deep breaths in and out. Timmy was holding on to the armrest on the door with both hands. He does not like high-stress situations. I think I'll get him a bowl after this to calm him down.

Mikey met us outside with a smile and open arms.

"Hello, boys!"

"What's up, Mikey?" I asked, still breathing hard form the race car driving clinic I just put on.

"Are we good?" he asked.

"Yep, right here." I patted the duffle bag and removed it from the truck.

We went into the garage with Mikey's direction and found there were more people inside now. Two young attractive women were sitting on the bed where the duffle bag full of drugs were. They were sitting against the headboard with pillows behind them and practically on each other's laps. Both were wearing string bikinis and hardly leaving anything to the imagination.

Timmy was fixated on the two women. And this was what Mikey wanted, for them to remove any concentration of the business deal. This was not going to work for me. Yes, they were beautiful and sexy, but I had a job to do. I needed to stay razor-sharp.

The music was loud, and the pot smoke was thick. Both women were sharing a joint, back and forth, back and forth. Probably the sexiest that I've ever seen anyone smoke anything. Before anyone could ask me if I wanted a hit from anything, I reached into my vest pocket and pulled out my pack of Marlboro Lights with my "special" cigarettes. I took out a joint and lit it.

"Now it's a party!" Mikey yelled over the music.

Mikey jumped onto the bed and squeezed in between the two girls. He took the joint from the one on the left and placed it in his lips, breathed in, and closed his eyes. He exhaled slow and smooth. I did the same with my joint. We both laughed.

Timmy had a look of bewilderment as he leaned against the refrigerator. He opened it and removed a bottle of Bud Light, twisted the cap off, and took a big pull off the brown bottle. His hands were wet from the condensation. He wiped his hands on his dirty pants, leaving a streak from his fingers. He continued to watch the two ladies, trying to get a glimpse of a nipple or side boob or anything.

Have you ever tried to get a child to leave Toys "R" Us when they don't want to? Well, that's what is going to be like getting Timmy to leave. If you saw Timmy's girlfriend, it would be comprehensible why he wants to stay. She is not an attractive girl.

We continued to listen to music, smoke marijuana, drink beer, and sneak glances of the two lovely ladies on the bed. I looked at my watch and realized we had been there for about an hour. I told Mikey that we needed to get going and to finish the deal.

"Ya, you guys have a long drive ahead of you. Let's get this done."

Mikey jumped off the bed and grabbed my duffle bag and unzipped it. He opened the bag and a smile encompassed his face.

"Is it all here?" he asked.

"Every cent."

"Fantastic!"

He threw me the bag with the drugs and told me to take a look. I was a little apprehensive and unzipped it carefully, closing one eye, like that would help if it blew up. I opened the bag and checked the product. All here.

"When would you like to meet up again, Preacher?"

"Let me get back to you. Do you know when you'll have more?"

"Now, I have more now. I always have something. Let me know what you want before you get here, and I'll tell ya if I got it."

There's no way this guy has this much all the time. Who is this guy?

"Cool, lemme get yer number and I'll reach out soon."

"Here ya go." Mikey handed me a piece of paper with two sets of numbers. Both cell phone numbers. He said to text the first one; if no response, text the second one. "These are burner phones, so the numbers will change soon."

"I get it."

I walked out the doors with the duffle bag in my hand and a contact buzz in my head. Timmy had drunk a few too many beers and also with a contact buzz, he was feeling pretty good right now and will need a nap soon.

Driving down the dark blacktop, my primary goal was to keep the pickup between the ditches. There were four center lines, and the speed I was traveling seemed to exceed the posted speed limit. However, unbeknownst to me, I was driving at about twenty miles an hour under the speed limit. Brandon, watching the driving exhibition, laughed the entire way, although hoping I would not crash with twenty-five thousand dollars' worth of drugs with me.

By the time we reached the sheriff's office, I was half asleep, and Timmy was passed out. Russ came down to meet us. I didn't get out of the truck and handed him the duffle bag. I rested my now-pounding head on my hand against the side of the door of the truck.

"Come on, man, get outta the truck. Leave him there and come upstairs so we can get this logged in." Russ ordered me.

Jason and Nick arrived a short time later and advised there were three more people who showed up after we left. They obtained the vehicle plate information and description of the people for the investigation. Tomorrow will be a better day to focus on the identity of those people. It's nappy time. I took a power nap on the office couch after I hid all the office Sharpies.

CHAPTER 17

I waited until the next Wednesday to contact Mikey. I figured if I contact him too soon, he will wonder how I'm getting rid of the drugs so fast and become suspicious. I sent him a text only saying, "Looking," while sitting at my home hanging out with my dog, Hemi, watching a ball game.

Hemi is a 180-pound Rottweiler. I rescued him from an animal shelter a few years ago; he is my best friend and support. Hemi is a very kind, loving dog. He sits with me, rides with me, and sleeps next to me. He howls to the song, "Girls, Girls, Girls," by Mötely Crüe, and he doesn't like shotguns or beer cans. I'm not sure what happened with his previous owner but judging by his reaction when he sees a Black man; his former owner was Black.

I had a friend of mine who didn't believe me that dogs can be racist. So, we tested it. He was an older Black man and we met in my garage. I explained to him I would hold the leash and not to make any sudden movements, which he agreed. I brought out Hemi. He sniffed around for a second, then saw my friend and aggressively barked, lunged, and showed his teeth. My buddy jumped on the work bench in case Hemi broke free. Our test proved it.

A short time later, I received a text response, "Here." I called Russ and told him we needed to set up another deal. He agreed, only he didn't want me to buy as much this time, which is typically the opposite of how controlled buys go. They usually increase with each purchase.

I called Timmy and told him to be ready to go in one hour. He complained and drug his feet until I explained to him that it wasn't a choice. I also told him he didn't need to go with me after this. He agreed to that.

An hour later, we met at our usual spot in the cemetery. It was warm again, humid, which makes everything sticky and damp. There was an overcast sky and rain in the forecast, enough to provide some relief. I threw Timmy's bike in the bed of the pickup, and we took off to meet with the team in Hastings. I hope it goes as smooth as the first one, without guns pointed at each other, of course.

When we arrived, we followed the protocol we set initially and drove to the sally port door to be let in. Once inside, we were to wait until met by one of the team members, which was usually Russ. Russ appeared, we exchanged pleasantries and jokes. He said hello to Timmy, which he has never done prior to today. I looked at Timmy and smiled. He rolled his eyes.

"Brandon, Nick and Jason are upstairs waiting for us." Russ informed.

"Any issues getting the cash?"

"Nope, we're good."

"Perfect."

We made our way through maze of offices in the sheriff's office and passed the dispatch center where there were two women with headsets on looking into computer screens and typing. One was a beautiful younger woman with blonde hair and pink sweatshirt. Her hair was up in a tight ponytail. Where have I seen her before?

She could not see me as I passed the glass partition. I peered over my shoulder squinting, thinking really hard…

I know her from somewhere…

"Hey, Russ, what's that dispatchers name, the one in the pink sweatshirt?"

"Sarah, why do you ask?"

"Fuck!" I said in a loud whisper as I grabbed a hold of Russ's arm and pulled him into an office that had the door opened.

"What the fuck, man?" he yelled, startled, as he looked down at his arm that I'm still holding on to.

"I know her!"

"So?"

"Naw, you don't get it. I bought dope from this dude Glenn, remember? At his house one night was Jeremy and *her*! She was there smoking weed and drinking wine coolers wearing that exact same sweatshirt! She knows who I am, well, who I'm not, I mean."

"Well, shit. This could be a problem."

"When does she get off shift?"

"Not till midnight."

"Can ya get her outta here b'fore that?"

"How the hell am I goin' to do that?"

"I don't know. Tell her you're not busy enough to have two dispatchers on. Will that work?"

"Okay, lemme check with something. Stay here, don't go wanderin' 'round. I don't want her ta see ya."

"Got it," I replied, closing the door behind Russ while he figured out the cluster fuck.

Murphy's law has reared its ugly head again and this time looking right through my soul.

Timmy and I hung out in the office waiting, going over every possible scenario that could transpire from this specific situation. Russ came back in with his head down. He removed his glasses and rubbed his eyes.

"I have an idea, but you ain't gonna like it."

I didn't answer. I waited for him to tell me the operation was over and we go home. He looked up and adjusted his holster.

"So, you saw Sarah smoking weed in this dude's house with that Jeremy kid, right?"

"Yep." I nodded in agreeance.

"Okay. Here's what I'm going to do… I'm goin' to bring her in and introduce you to her. If she recognizes you, I'll either fire her or she can work with us."

"That's the option? Really? That's the best you can come up with? Good Lord!"

"Gimmee a minute."

Russ left the office and returned a minute later. When he entered the room, he wasn't alone; Sarah, the dispatcher was right behind him with her head down. I was sitting on the corner of the large wooden desk, trying to not knock off the pictures and disrupt the papers. She looked up and startled, trying to turn around and leave. Russ stopped her and told her to come in and have a seat.

"Hello, Sarah, remember me?" I asked, already knowing the answer.

She nodded her head, trying not to make eye contact. I crouched down in attempt to gain her attention.

"Where do you know me from?" I asked.

"Glenn's."

"Right. Glenn's. What were you doing there?"

She did not answer.

"Answer him," Russ told her in the voice of a boss.

"I was there with Jeremy, and we were just having some fun, you know."

Sarah was sobbing now, trying to hold her composure. She wiped her tears with her sleeve where her hand was tucked into.

"Yes, Sarah, I do know. I was there, remember?"

"Ya, well, you were smokin' weed too! I saw you. Don't pretend you're better than me!" she blurted out.

"Unfortunately for you, the weed I was smoking was fake, and the weed you were smokin' was real. I'd be real careful how you want to go about this. Yer the one on the hot seat not me. I'm trying to help you, by you helping me."

"Ya? How can I do that?"

"Yer goin' to identify the people we can't. Yer goin' to be our inside man, I mean woman."

"Or what? If I don't help you?" she asked.

"Russ, I'll let you answer that one."

"Sarah, you are going to be suspended for unbecoming a law enforcement officer. You are going to help them with whatever they need, then when the operation is over, you will be reinstated as a dispatcher. Or you can be charged and fired right now. Your decision."

She contemplated about it for a few minutes. Internally, she weighed her options. The idea of being charged and fired for one night of fun did not sound pleasing to her. What would her family think? How would she finish her degree? She was not excited about the options and rightfully so. But she put herself in this situation.

"What's it goin' ta be?" I asked.

"Fine. How can I help?"

"That's what I wanted to hear! Great!"

I asked Russ to step out in the hallway with me for a minute. Timmy and Sarah sat in the deputy's office while we conversed.

"He's a dick, ain't he?" Timmy confirmed with Sarah.

"Ya, he really is," she replied, wiping her eyes and nose.

I asked Russ if we identified all the others who had been frequenting Mikey and Jeremy's. He said they had not. I asked him to show Sarah the pictures and find out who they were, and we would get the operation rolling again for tonight but take her phone from her and keep her in sight until we are finished for the night. He agreed. I reentered the office and removed Timmy to meet with the team in the conference room and explain what just happened.

After explaining the whole Sarah thing with the team, they all looked at Nick and busted out laughing. I didn't need to ask; I already knew the history between Nick and Sarah without hearing details. I did ask Nick if it was over, he assured me it was and permanently. I gave Russ the photos of the people we needed to identify to show Sarah. As a group, we then went over the operation order for the night. I requested Brandon to take over this portion to keep things consistent. Timmy sat in the big comfortable office chair confused as ever.

CHAPTER 18

After getting all the gear together and the buy money, we left the conference room and went to the sally port to get the pickup ready for another drug buy. I always go over every inch of the truck to make sure all is functioning correctly, trying to stay one step ahead of Murphy and his dumbass laws. To help keep track of my truck better at night, I drilled a hole in the left taillight to emit a little white light. It's just enough for the cover officer to see when behind, but not enough for someone to recognize when the lights are not on.

I checked the air pressure in the tires, the fluids, the headlights, and bright and low beams. I made sure my backup pistol was accessible and hidden in the seat crack on my left side. I keep it there in the event I need to shoot someone to my right and my right hand is unavailable. Also, the boot knife stashed in the visor is still there, check.

I'm only buying three pounds of marijuana tonight, so I only have three thousand dollars. Nicely wrapped in a brown paper bag and stowed under my seat. That's a lot different than the twenty-five thousand that I had last week. I texted Mikey and told him I would be there sometime tonight. I don't like to give a specific time because I don't want them to set up an ambush. Just giving the time frame is dangerous enough, at least this way it keeps them guessing.

I turned onto Highway 20 and drove east. There was not much traffic as it was close to ten o'clock at night. As we were driving, a car approached and passed, then made a U-turn in the middle of the highway. An Iowa state trooper was about to stop me or hopefully just needed to change directions quickly and was responding to a call and won't bother with me.

Well, I was wrong, he's stopping me. He activated his emergency red and blue lights along with his wigwags. I slowed down to pull off the roadway onto the shoulder. I told Timmy to keep his mouth shut and not say a word. Timmy was giggling at this point. I gave him the hairy stink eye and waited for the kind trooper to approach the driver's side.

I rolled the window down manually. I don't think 1976 Ford pickups had electric windows yet. I replaced my hands at the "ten and two" position on the steering wheel awaiting orders. The flashlight ricocheting off the mirror blinded me. He suddenly appeared next to me at the "B" pillar.

"License, registration, and proof of insurance." The trooper matter-of-factly ordered.

"Yes, sir. I have my license here in my wallet that I will reach for now."

I needed to be careful how I go about this as I have three thousand dollars under the seat and, more importantly, a Glock in the small of my back. I retrieved my wallet and unzipped the secured pocket to get out my fake driver's license. I explained to him that my registration and insurance was in my glove compartment and reached over to open it. And then I heard it...

"Don't you fuckin' move, asshole! Show me yer hands! Now!"

Oh boy, this is going to go badly, I thought to myself.

I obeyed the trooper and did not move. My door opened, and I felt this hand on the back of my neck and squeezed. The trooper pulled me out of the truck like he has done a hundred times to others and put me face down on the gravel surface of the shoulder. He grabbed ahold of my pistol by the grip and yanked it out of my waistband. He stood upright with his sidearm pointed at Timmy and his boot in the middle of my back.

"Don't you fuckin' move, boy!" I'm not sure if he was talking to Timmy or me, but neither of us moved.

"Sir, sir, if you let me explain, you'll see that this is a big misunderstanding."

"Shut tha fuck up!"

"Okay," I said under my breath.

My phone in my pocket was ringing; of course, I had no way to find out who it was. I figured it was Brandon or Mikey. But why Brandon didn't come up to help me, I won't find out until later. The trooper handcuffed me behind my back and stood me up. He walked me to the front bumper of his squad car and told me to sit, which I did.

"Pale Riders, huh? Who tha fuck is that? You a new club tryin' to move into my territory? You fuckin' bikers are all the same, a bunch of scumbags. Every chance I get, I will put you in jail. Now what ya doin' here, boy?"

"Well, sir, yer gonna laugh, but I'm on the job. I'm workin' up here and you see that car sittin' back there? That's my cover officer."

"Oh, bullshit! That's the dumbest thing I ever heard!"

"Well, that may be, but it's true."

"Who do you work for then?"

"I'm workin' with the Hastings Drug Task Force, and Brandon is my cover officer. That guy in the passenger seat is my CI. And I'm goin' to be needin' my gun back so I can complete my mission."

I could see the expression on this trooper's face become sheepish and a little annoyed. Brandon pulled up and approached us.

"Don't shoot, I'm a cop," he announced as he walked along the highway.

"You know this guy?" the Trooper asked Brandon.

"Unfortunately, yes."

"Kiss my ass." I quipped.

The trooper looked me up and down and shook his head. He reached into his right front pants pocket, retrieved a handcuff key, and told me to turn around. He was kind enough to unlock the cuffs for me. I rubbed my wrists to ease the pain.

He handed me my Glock politely. I ejected the magazine and checked the chamber, then inserted the mag and replaced it in the small of my back.

"Man, I would never guess you a cop. I guaran-damn-tee the bad guys won't either. Good on you, son."

And with that, he entered his squad car, turned off his overhead lights, and left with a wave out the window.

Once the kind trooper had left, we continued with the mission to buy weed from Mikey and Jeremy. Brandon returned to his vehicle and I to mine. I entered the pickup and sat down and waited a moment to collect my thoughts and get my mind right.

Timmy broke the silence and said, "Well, that was fun. Let's do that again."

I shook my head in derision and turned the key in the ignition. I had to wait until my eyes adjusted to the dark and then pulled out onto the highway to head to the brother's trailer. Brandon's headlights shown through the rear window of the truck until I pulled far enough ahead that they were no longer visible.

Jason and Nick patiently waited until we arrived, twenty minutes later than expected. They were in contact with Brandon and gave the "all clear" signal to proceed with the meet. We entered Wolf Park, and it was darker than usual. No one was moving around, and there were minimal lights on. No vehicles and no loud music. A little odd but nothing stood out that said not to continue.

I stopped the truck a trailer away from Jeremy and Mikey's. I paused, looked, and listened. My cover team can hear me, but I can't hear them.

"I don't like this," I said into the mic.

Timmy and I walked to their trailer, the loose gravel under my boots crunching with every step until I reached their dirt "yard" then became soft underfoot. I could taste the dust as it floated around in the cool summer breeze. One light cast a shadow to the entry way of the garage where we were supposed to meet.

I stood still for a moment listening, letting my eyes readjust, focus. A faint conversation coming from the interior of the garage told me there were more than one person, not an issue. A slight smell of cigarette smoke emanated from the cracks of the door and windows.

I knocked on the door with a rhythmic beat, a knock that doesn't say I'm a cop. Law enforcement have a very distinct knock, one that is not gentle. I've actually broken a window with my knocking, by accident, of course.

Jeremy answered the door. He didn't say a word, just turned around and waved us in. We entered the garage walk-in door and stood by the refrigerator. Timmy by my side like a child, afraid to leave his father in a crowd. Mikey sat on the edge of the neatly made bed, wrinkling the dark blue comforter. A 1911-style pistol in his right hand resting on his thigh. Hammer cocked and safety engaged.

"Here we go again," Timmy said, exhausted of this repeated situation.

"What's goin' on, Mikey?" I asked, not looking forward to this song and dance after the last go around.

"I dunno, bro, you tell me."

"I have no idea what tha fuck yer talkin' about, dude."

"Ya wanna tell me about the state trooper ya met tonight?"

"That? Man, I got pulled over for a busted taillight. That's it."

"Troopers don't point their guns at ya for a busted taillight."

"Ha ha ha! Ya, yer right. They don't, but he thought I was some dude that had a warrant out for him for assault. That's all that was, mistaken identity." I did my best "Aw shucks, Eddie Haskell" impression as I explained the traffic stop to the room.

"You sure?"

"Ya, man, that's it. Otherwise, I wouldn't be here right now. Right?"

In my mind, I was making sense; I hoped I was making sense. But I was trying to negotiate with a doper and someone holding a gun with a lot to lose if I were to narc on him to the cops.

"Right." Mikey agreed.

I changed the subject seamlessly by throwing him the brown paper bag with the three thousand dollars, which he caught one handed. Another White male sat on the couch next to Jeremy whom I did not know. I didn't see a car or motorcycle outside. Maybe I could sneak a photo with my phone, but I haven't mastered that technique yet.

Mikey stood up and went to the dresser and removed a blue duffle bag with three pounds of marijuana from the bottom drawer and threw it to me.

"Here, have fun, bro."

"Thanks! We got a couple minutes, ya mind if I light up?" I asked, trying to stall to figure out who the other guy is.

"I got shit to do, some other time, man. Text me next week."

And with that, we left. Once we got into the truck, I asked Timmy if he had any idea who that was on the couch. He said no, and he had never seen him before.

Driving down the highway to return to the sheriff's office, I decided to take an alternate route, one that we determined as route number two, just to make sure no one follows me. It's a little out of the way, but if someone is following me, this route will indicate it.

I called Brandon and told him about the unknown male, which he relayed the message to the other guys, who stated they did not see anyone out of the ordinary enter the garage.

The coast was clear all the way to the sheriff's office where we pulled into the sally port to log in evidence. This stuff really smelled like high-quality weed, not that local ditch weed shit. This might be BC Bud (British Columbia Bud). I couldn't imagine getting pulled over with this smell, radiating from the cab of the truck. Even a rookie cop could recognize this smell.

We documented all the information regarding tonight's controlled buy and added to the charges we will soon be laying on these guys and girls. This will be one hell of a case by the time it's all said and done. I still needed to buy from Jeremy and their stepdad, James. It would be nice to file federally under the RICO Act, but I don't know if that will be possible at this time.

CHAPTER 19

The next week, I thought I would amp it up with Mikey. I had already bought a shit ton of drugs from him and intend on buying more. The more I buy, the more drugs removed from the streets. I needed some guns. Let's see what kind of guns I can buy.

I texted Mikey one afternoon and asked him to call me when he got a chance. He didn't respond by text, he called immediately.

"You clear to talk?" I asked Mikey on the phone.

"Yep, what is going on?"

"I need something. Something more than what I had bought before."

"You want more?" Emphasized "more."

"No. Well, yes, but also need some protection. We've got some issues with some southern hombres, if you know what I mean."

"Yep, I can do that. How about military M4s?"

I paused and held my hand over my mouth to stifle a joy of adulation.

"Really? That would be awesome! Mags and ammo, too?"

"Yep, I got a crate already to go. A grand for each."

"When can I get it?"

"How soon can you be here?"

"Three hours, bro."

"Done, see you then."

I hung up. Holy shit! A crate of military M4 rifles, no "fing" way! I am surely going to get officer of the year this time!

I did not work as an undercover operative for the accolades. I did it because it's the best job in law enforcement in my opinion. Being a law enforcement officer is not done for the money or adulations; it is done to make the communities safe and to help the public get rid of crime. But I got to say the feeling of buying kilos of meth, pounds of marijuana, and a bunch of illegal guns from bad guys is a feeling like none other.

I gotta call Russ!

"Rusty! Yer not goin' to believe this shit! B'fore you try to guess, I'll just tell ya. I called Mikey, and he's got a crate of M4s he wants to get rid of. One grand a gun. Let's do this!"

"Whoa, slow down, brother. We need to talk."

"Talk? Talk 'bout what?"

"It looks as if the Feds got wind of the work you been puttin' in, and they want in."

"Nope, fuck that, not happenin'. This is my case, our case, not theirs. Let them do their own work on their own cases."

"Come in so we can talk about this, Phil."

"Russ, there's nothin' to talk 'bout. I ain't givin' this to them."

"Just come in."

"Fine, I'll be there in an hour. But I'm standin' by what I said."

I hung up and slammed my phone on the couch. Thankfully, it was the couch; otherwise, it would have broken, and I wouldn't have a way to call Mikey. I got dressed and headed to Hastings to meet with Russ. I called Brandon on the way and told him what I found with Mikey and the Feds issue. He told me he would meet me at the sheriff's office and help sort this out.

When I arrived, Russ, Brandon, and an agent with the ATF, Agent Johnson, were waiting for me in the sally port. I turned the ignition off and stared straight ahead. Russ opened the truck door for me and proceeded to introduce me to Agent Johnson. I politely shook his outreached hand in a kind but meaningless gesture.

"Phil, Agent Johnson is here to assist us in the case with Mikey and his family."

I released Agent Johnson's grip and put my hands in my pocket to wipe off the betrayal and condensation.

Agent Johnson stood there in his government-issued dark blue suit and red breakaway tie, with black sensible shoes. The dimly lit garage provided a single light bulb glare off his freshly shaved head. His neatly trimmed goatee annoyed me that he was able to maintain his hygiene and appearance while I looked like someone living in the gutters.

"Officer Quick, I am only here to help with the investigation against Mikey, not take it over. We can use our resources and personnel to take these dregs of society down and put them away for a long time."

Agent Johnson's tongue was even government-issued with his fancy talk and proper English. To address me as

Officer Quick was odd as I do not look like an officer of the law. And it irritated me. Without saying a word, I looked at Russ as if to say, *You need to step up and stop this before I say something that will get me fired.* Russ understood and stepped in.

"Agent Johnson, we appreciate you taking your time to come up here on a hot summer day, but we do have this handled. But if you were to help, what could you do that has not already been done?" Russ asked ever so politely.

"Ya, I'm curious, too. What can you do that I haven't? I mean, I bought dope from these guys an' generated trust to the point that I can show up anytime and buy whatever I want, can you?"

"No, I cannot do that. We still need you to do the buys and then introduce an agent to them so we can figure out where they are getting the rifles from."

How the hell does he know about the rifles already?

"So, you want me to introduce an agent to Mikey? Nope, not happenin' brah."

"Phil, hold on. Let's think about this." Russ tried to calm me down and convince me this was a good idea.

"So, here's how this is goin' down. I take an ATF agent with me to a buy of which I have not done myself, and hope, *hope*, Mikey and Jeremy don't get spooked and shoot me. He's already pointed a gun at me twice. He's too unstable for me to introduce another dude." I explained the whole scene to all who would listen.

I leaned up against the rear quarter panel of my truck and lit a Marlboro red cigarette. Russ glared at me for smoking in the garage. Brandon started laughing.

"Look, guys, I need to get to Mikey's so I can buy some guns. You got my back on this?" I asked Russ and Brandon, not caring what Agent Johnson thought.

"Ya, let's get this done, and then we can discuss it more when we're done," Russ grudgingly stated.

Agent Johnson interjected and asked about a big player in the area associated with a new outlaw motorcycle club.

"Are you familiar with a White male, who goes by 'Preacher'? He's in his midthirties and built like a linebacker in football. He has a shaved head and a long goatee and is throwing around a lot of money, according to my source."

As he was describing this 'Preacher' character, he was looking down in a government-issued black notebook with a fancy file folder, all the while we were looking at him and at each other in confusion—confusion that he is a Federal law enforcement agent and the fact the person he was describing was standing five feet from him.

"Is this guy serious?" I asked with a look of condensation.

Russ stopped him and me (from putting my foot in my mouth).

"Sir, they are giving you information regarding Officer Quick. The person you are describing is him." He pointed at me as he finished his sentence.

"I see." Agent Johnson felt a little embarrassed at this point and rightfully so. "Well, I will pass this information along. You're doing a fine job, Officer Quick."

I nodded in appreciation. The unknown guy sitting on the couch with Jeremy the other night is a federal snitch, good to know.

The case of M4 rifles, mags, and ammunition is going to cost twenty-four thousand dollars since there are twenty-four rifles per case. Where in the hell did he get a case of M4s? I can't wait to ask him, but I will find out soon enough.

I suited up with all my equipment, still fuming form the bullshit conversation that I just had. I need to stop and get my head right. Actually, this anger might help. Let's do this!

Jason and Nick were already in position. I conducted a comm check with Brandon. Agent Johnson tagged along with Brandon as my cover, cover officer. I'd love to be a fly in that vehicle listening to their conversation.

I pulled into the trailer park and stopped the truck in front of Mikey's trailer. He exited the garage and made his way to the passenger side of my truck. He jumped in and made himself as comfortable as he could.

"Jesus Christ! What a piece of shit!"

"Ya thanks, maybe someday when I get my credit score up, I can go buy a new one, asshole."

"Ha, ha, ha! Let's go. When you get out on the highway, turn right."

"Where we goin', bro?"

"Yer on a need-to-know basis."

"Well, I kinda need to know since I'm drivin'."

"Ha, true! Okay, go to the Army National Guard base."

"How the hell we gettin' on the base?"

"Don't worry about it, dude. I got this."

We drove south for about four miles and approached the army base where there was a guard shack with two sentries and a wood arm guard blocking the roadway. As we approached one sentry, armed with an M4 rifle slung across his chest and a 9mm Beretta M9 pistol in a green holster on his right hip. His army BDUs neatly pressed and his maroon beret crisp and covering his left eye.

He put up his left arm and held his hand out flat, palm outward to signal us to stop while his right hand slid to the pistol grip of the M4 and curled his fingers around except his trigger finger. It stayed straight along the trigger guard as he was trained.

I stopped the truck at the white line on the road that said "Stop."

"State your business, sir," The guard said in a military manner that brought me back to my Marine Corps days. Of course, I did it much better, but it's not a competition.

Mikey leaned toward me and said, "We're here to see Sgt. First Class Raburn in supply."

"Stand by one."

The guard did an about face and stepped into the guard shack where he picked up a military phone and proceeded to talk with someone. Mikey still leaning on to my side of the truck waiting for a response. The guard returned and asked if we knew where to go. Mikey told him we did. The wooden guard arm raised, and we drove forward. The level of confusion and curiosity was beyond any that I had experienced since beginning this operation.

Mikey sat on his side of the truck with a satisfied smirk while moving his head back and forth with the beat of the music on the radio. He pointed to a brick, one-story building that looked exactly like all the other brick, one-story buildings on base.

"This is it, dude. I should have asked this before we left, but do you have the money?"

"Uh, ya," was all I could get out.

"Cool, let's go."

I followed Mikey to the door of the building that said "Base Supply," below that, "Sgt. First Class Raburn." Mikey knocked and walked in, didn't wait for an invitation.

"Raburn!" he called out.

"Back here!"

We made our way passed the offices and into a large room with hard case after hard case of military equipment stacked floor to ceiling. Raburn was behind a steel cage placing M4 rifles into a large OD green Pelican case. It sat upon another Pelican case, which contained all the magazines and ammunition.

"Raburn, this is my boy, Preacher. This shit is for him and his crew."

"I don't need to know where it's going. Ya got the money?"

"Show him the money, Preacher."

I dropped the duffle bag with twenty-four thousand dollars on the floor in front of the cage door. He looked down through the steel mesh and waited for me to open it. I unzipped the bag and pried it open so he could see in. I moved the stacks of one-hundred-dollar bills around so he could see they were all there.

"Great, come around to the other side." He pointed to his right where there was a steel roll up door.

The Pelican cases were on a flat dolly with four cast wheels, which made it easy to push to the truck. Once we got them to the truck, we picked up the cases and placed them in the back next to each other and strapped them down with motorcycle tie-downs. The last thing I wanted was the cases to fly out while driving down the highway. We exchanged pleasantries and left the base.

I waved to the sentries as I passed the guard shack as a gesture of thanks for your service. The whole time, I'm thinking, *I have a shit load of stolen guns and ammo from the government in the back of my pickup. This is crazy!*

I dropped Mikey off at his trailer and told him I needed to get these back to the club ASAP. Plus, I did not want to go in the garage and hang out while the guns are sitting in the back of the truck unattended. How would I explain that if they were stolen?

I returned to the sheriff's office and drove into the sally port where Russ was waiting for me. He was standing in the middle of the garage and had to back up as I pulled in. His hands in his pockets of his dark gray dress pants fidgeting with spare coins and keys.

"What's up, boss?" I asked.

"Did you get them?"

"Of course, twenty-four rifles and a lot of mags and ammo. Let's look."

I jumped into the back of the pickup and put on two latex gloves. I opened the front case and sure enough, twenty-four government-issued M4 rifles, nicely stacked in their respective locked slot. I opened the next container and half was stacked thirty-round metal magazines, and the other half was multiple boxes of fifty-five grain ball ammo. A polymer partition separated the mags and ammo. I never expected to get something like this. These guns were going to go to real bad people to do real bad things.

I helped carry the containers upstairs where we will spend the next couple hours logging in all the evidence to continue stockpiling conspiracy charges on Mikey and now a member of the armed services, Sgt. First Class Raburn.

CHAPTER 20

During the months of buying drugs every week from Mikey and Jeremy, I did end up buying from both Jeremy and his stepdad, James. Small quantities of marijuana and meth, but they were purchases and would count toward the investigation of conspiracy to deliver controlled substances. In Iowa, the amount does not dictate for the level of charge. A sale is a sale. Under the Iowa Code Section 124.401, they were to be charged with felony distribution charges as well. The count now is Mikey, Jeremy, and James, as well as Sgt. First Class Raburn.

Timmy called me one day to let me know he was contacted by a Laotian man he used to work with who was trying to unload some meth. He, too, lives in Hastings, by the fairgrounds, which is literally the opposite side of town that Jeremy and Mikey live.

David lives in a quadplex across from the county fairgrounds. The quadplex is a two-story, four-apartment complex, which was once an office building and now converted into low-rent apartments. The building looks as if it were built in the early 1900s. Its main door is at the top of six concrete stairs leading from the wide sidewalk. Ornate swirls and designs encase a Latin saying decorate above the doorway from a distant time.

A large wooden sign posted in the front yard "Welcome to Pleasant View Apartments" looked out of place with the style of the building. Green and light brown grass surrounded the complex as it sat by itself in the center of the block. A "No Pets" sign stuck to the front door rounded out the dueling time period motif of the apartment.

David told Timmy to show up around 5:00 p.m., and he would run it out to him. He told Timmy he would sell a "ball" for three hundred dollars. Timmy agreed before letting me know, but we would make it work.

I met with Timmy in our usual spot and threw "his" bike in the back of the truck. Before he sat down in the trucks seat, he removed a sixteen-ounce bottle of Mountain Dew from his back pocket. I have never put a soda bottle in my back pocket while riding a bike, but I can't imagine it being very comfortable. He twisted open the sweaty Mountain Dew bottle and took a pull, closing his eyes in satisfaction.

Such a simple person, Timmy is.

As we ventured down the county blacktop heading to make another drug buy, I clarified with Timmy how he knew David and needed more information about him and who he's associated with. Timmy didn't have a lot of information other than they worked together for a brief time at the West Star Company, then he moved to Hastings with his family and got a job in a factory there.

I asked about his family; he said David was married and had one fourteen-year-old son, David Junior. They called him DJ. *Makes sense*, I thought.

Timmy didn't know where David got his meth, but he usually had some. My concern was that David called Timmy out of the blue and told him that he had some to unload. Tweakers are unpredictable and are generally difficult to read. The things that make sense to them don't make sense to normal people who don't use drugs. Still, my antennas were raised and senses on high alert.

I contacted Brandon and Russ and explained what was going on. They both told me they knew who he was, and they have been trying to get him busted for a year or so when they first heard of him. One thing they expressed was to be careful because he does like to carry a .22-caliber pocket pistol. Does every scumbag in this town carry a gun?

We met in the sally port at the sheriff's office; at which time, they handed me the documented three hundred dollars. Knowing what I know about the drug trade in the Midwest, this is not going to be high quality meth. But that doesn't matter. It's getting put into evidence, not into my body. When it comes to the illegal distributing of drugs, the quality does not matter. In fact, in Iowa, when a drug dealer portrays the substance to be drugs and sells it to another, it is still a felony. Crazy, I know, but it is what it is.

I installed the mic in my vest and double-checked all my equipment as I have done numerous times before an operation commenced. A comm check functioned correctly, and the weather was clear; no wind, no rain. So far so good, the law of Murphy has not reared its ugly head. Good to go.

Timmy and I proceeded to the apartment complex through the busy downtown of Hastings, passing the local restaurants and secondhand stores, hardware stores, and beautiful landscaping. The downtown was the pride of Hastings. This really would be a nice place to live, except for the drug problem of course. But we're working on that.

I turned onto Cedar Street and approached the entrance of the county fairgrounds. I changed it up for a moment and turned into the front entrance of the vacant fairgrounds and drove through the livestock housing area. I stopped and got out to pee. Once I was done, Timmy asked me why I didn't go to the sheriff's office or a gas station. I shrugged him off. I didn't tell Timmy everything about what I do or how I conduct my business.

What I was really doing was trying to assess the situation in the event I was being set up. I paused to smell the flowers, so to say. Things were going too smoothly, and I didn't like it. I did not do any homework on David, and I was concerned with the unknown.

We drove along the dirt road to the entrance of the fairgrounds to leave and buy some meth. The road was inline and across the street with the front of the apartment complex. A lone individual was sitting on the top step of the front stairs. As I got closer, I could tell it was a teenage Asian boy.

"That's DJ." Timmy pointed out.

"Fourteen, ya say?"

"Ya, I think so."

"I bet he has the shit and is going to sell it to us."

"Why do ya say that?" Timmy questioned.

"Sending a juvenile to commit a felony, they get less time. Especially if Dad is already a felon, less risk for him," I explained.

Sure enough, I was right. I stopped in front of the apartment complex facing the direction of oncoming traffic. Fortunately, it was not a busy street. DJ bound off the steps and jogged to us. His right hand balled in a fist, his left hand empty. His shaggy, black hair bouncing with every step. He stopped at the truck and completely ignored me.

"Timmy?"

"Yep."

DJ held his hand outstretched in the cab of the truck in front of me and produced an eight ball of light brown powder in a plastic baggie, cinched tight with a rubber band. I put the three hundred dollars cash in my interior vest pocket prior to us stopping and handed him the money after I took the baggie of meth. He didn't say a word, turned and jumped up the steps, and disappeared in the building.

I looked at Timmy. He shrugged his shoulders in uncertainty. I shook my head and put the truck in gear. We returned to the sheriff's office and met Brandon and Russ in the sally port.

"What tha fuck was that?" I exclaimed.

"That was the easiest buy I've ever seen," Brandon said in amazement.

"Too easy," I replied, looking for Murphy.

I handed Brandon the baggie of meth and told him I would email him my report.

"Wanna get supper?" he asked.

"Sure, yer buyin'."

I bought three more times from DJ during the next few weeks. All four times, I bought an eight ball of meth. All in the same manner, DJ would meet me outside, and we would exchange money for drugs. This was the easiest transaction I conducted but very effective. All were the same grade and quality. I did not know where they were getting it from, but I know they were debriefed after they were arrested for distribution. Some cases were continued without my assistance, which was totally fine with me. I had other jobs that I needed to finish as well.

And yes, Dad, David, did get arrested for child endangerment and coercing a child to commit a felony along with distribution charges and felon in possession of a firearm, which was a nice thing about Iowa in the early 2000s—the laws were very law enforcement friendly.

CHAPTER 21

Sarah proved to be quite useful with the information she provided. Not only did she identify numerous people, but also she gave up information on a pharmacist that was selling prescription drugs from his pharmacy in downtown Hastings.

Dr. James Quinn has been a pharmacist for approximately fifteen years and is the head pharmacist at the Regal Drugstore on Second Street. According to Sarah, Dr. Quinn became indebted to the Sons of Violence MC due to a prostitution addiction. He would provide pseudoephedrine pills, oxycodone, OxyContin, Percocet, and morphine to the club in exchange for leniency of the money owed. Brandon and I decided to pay the good doctor a visit at his drugstore one summer morning.

Brandon and I arrived at the Regal Drugstore at about 7:45 a.m. and knocked on the door. The cardboard white with red lettering "Closed" sign hanging from a white string was still visible in the front door. I put my face to the window and peered in, cupping my hands around my eyes to block the glare off the glass. One lone light on in the back of the store illuminating the counter where the controlled narcotics were stored. Brandon knocked on the glass again but harder.

Dr. Quinn emerged from the back, wiping his hands with a paper towel. He shook his head and waved his hand at us indicating he's not open yet. I motioned for him to come to the door. He again shook his head and pointed to his watch. I assumed that meant he didn't open for fifteen more minutes. He turned and disappeared through a door, presumably his office. Brandon and I waited. I strolled down the sidewalk to look around. I didn't go to Hastings often other than to buy drugs, so I haven't seen much of the beautiful downtown that was boasted about. There appeared to be a lovely diner across the street that was omitting a fantastic onslaught of breakfast aromas.

Great, now I'm hungry.

I made my way back to the drugstore where Brandon was sitting on the window ledge looking at his hands, lost in his nothingness thoughts.

"Almost eight." I informed Brandon.

"Yep," he replied nonchalantly.

He's not a man of many words.

I heard the doors deadbolt lock clank and the open doorbell chime as I turned to see Dr. Quinn flipping the sign to "Open."

"How can I help you, fellas?"

"I need some cold medicine," I replied, faking a sniffle.

"Well, come on in. It's at the front of the store by the register. We have to keep our eyes on it these days, if you know what I mean."

I did know what he meant, but I played it off that I didn't. I think I missed my calling as an actor. I would have made a great bad guy in an action movie...maybe someday.

Dr. Quinn was in his early fifties and bald on top with light brown hair around his head. He was approximately five feet, nine inches tall and heavyset. Not fat but frumpy. He walked with a pronounce pigeon step and kind of reminded me of a nerdy penguin from Batman and Robin. He wore his normal pharmacist uniform of khaki pleated pants, a checkered button-down shirt, and white lab coat.

I made my way through the store and located the shelf with the various cold medicine packages. I rummaged through the assortment cold medicines and found the brand that looked like it would work fine. There were five packs left of the type that I picked. I took all five to the counter, knowing I could only purchase two. It was the new law in Iowa that a person can only buy two packs of any medicine with pseudoephedrine in it. I placed all five packs on the counter and reached for my wallet.

"Oh, sir, sorry to inform you that you cannot buy five, you may only buy two. Leave the other three here and I'll return them to the shelf," Dr, Quinn explained the reason for the limit of packs.

"I see. Well, that's very disappointing."

Brandon took about five steps back and stood at the end of an aisle using it as cover while he removed his pistol from his waistband.

"I'm looking to get about one thousand pseudo pills," I explained, placing both of my hands flat on the counter in front of me and staring into Dr. Quinn's eyes.

"Oh, that's not possible. You see, sir, there are laws and regulations that I, we, must abide by. I could lose my license."

"We don't want that, do we?" I looked over my left shoulder to Brandon.

"Nope," he replied, man of few words.

"I have an obligation with some people you are associated with, and I need to get one thousand pills, or I can go and have a chat with the brothers at the club, if you know what I mean."

Dr. Quinn did know what I meant, and his look of sincerity turned to disdain.

"Wait here."

Dr. Quinn stepped out from behind the counter and walked to the front door, passing Brandon who had concealed his gun behind his thigh. He made his way to the door as a patron was entering. Dr. Quinn stopped him and asked that he come back in thirty minutes because he was finishing up the inventory. He promised a discount for the inconvenience. Dr. Quinn relocked the door and turned the sign to "Closed."

"One thousand, really? This is going to cost you, guys. That's almost my entire inventory."

"Okay, how much?" I asked.

"A grand, one dollar a pill."

"A *grand?*"

He nodded his head and looked back and forth from me to Brandon in anticipation. Dr. Quinn removed his glasses and placed them in his lab coat breast pocket. I didn't know if he thought he was about to get punched or he just didn't need them anymore.

"Fine, a thousand dollars. That's awful steep, but I get it."

"Do you have the money with you now?"

"Yes, sir."

"Good. Come with me to the back."

We followed Dr. Quinn to the back storage room where all the pharmacy supplies and new shipments arrive. It appears to be approximately thirty by thirty feet and has a walk-in door to the outside loading dock next to a garage door where the shipments get dropped off. The room was dimly lit unless the bay door was open. A security camera faced the location of the doors but was inoperable and there for show. The floors have chipped gray paint and were dusty with tracks from a pallet jack in organized tire patterns from the bay door to the interior walls. This really was not a secure area for the type of drugs stored. I made that comment to Dr. Quinn. He shrugged and said it's not his problem.

We followed him to the wall farthest from the doors where numerous brown boxes with medical terms and logos printed to signify which pharmaceutical company he chose to buy from. The boxes were stacked six feet high and in organization by sizes, large to small. He moved two middle boxes and reached in and pulled out a box about one foot by one foot, securely taped across the seams and edges with white pharmaceutical company tape. He turned and handed it to me.

"One thousand pseudoephedrine pills like you requested."

"Just like that?"

"Just like that... Now, I need my end."

"Oh, ya, sure, here you go." I handed him the one grand that I had folded and placed in my pocket.

Each bill marked and documented prior to our arrival this morning.

Now the dilemma is, do we bust him now or wait and do this again? I feel if we wait, we will be able to use the multiple deals against him in an airtight conviction. But if we bust him now, we can find out all the people he is selling to and break up his operation now, if he's willing to talk.

Let's wait.

As we walked out of the pharmacy, Brandon flipped the "Closed" sign back to "Open" and turned to Dr. Quinn to smirk in a smart-ass expression. The door closed behind us with a thud and the chime of the bell. As we walked down the sidewalk to the truck, a White male in his thirties wearing dark-colored clothing almost bumped into me. I excused myself and heard him mumble something in turn. He spun sideways to his left, pulled out his cell phone, and flipped it open. He pointed the back of the phone at us and a flash went off and then another.

"Hey! Did you just take our picture of us? Come 'ere!" I shouted in an authoritative voice.

The unidentified male flipped me off and turned to run. My initial reaction was to give chase, which was what Brandon was already doing. I followed Brandon the best that I could, but I am nowhere the speed demon that Brandon is. I once saw him run a mile on a high school track in full police uniform, vest, belt, and boots in under seven minutes.

The male opened a door and ran up the stairs with Brandon hot on his trail. I ran around the corner at the end of the block to cut him off in the back. I figured he was either running into an apartment on the second floor, or he was running across to get to the back where he had a car parked. Door number 2 was correct. He sprinted and bounded down the stairs, clearly running faster, scared that Brandon could catch up.

As soon as he broke through the door, I yelled for him to stop. The male reached into his front waistband, pulled out a black revolver, and pointed it at me. As soon as Brandon busted through the door, the man turned and fired twice, missing Brandon as he dove for cover off the concrete steps.

I fired my Glock at the male, striking him in the chest twice and the left shoulder twice. The revolver slid across the pavement as he crumpled to the sidewalk. Blood began to flow from under his body to the curb and into the street.

"You good?" I called out to Brandon.

"Yep," he replied, dusting himself off as he walked to the dying unidentified man.

"What tha fuck was that all about?"

"I dunno, let's see who this asshole is."

Brandon checked for the man's pulse that was now vacant. Then investigated his identity by searching for identification. I called 911 to request assistance and a coroner.

It's only eight forty-five in the morning!

CHAPTER 22

The next week, I met with Timmy at our usual location, the cemetery. I watched Timmy peddle his little heart out down the white rock path toward my truck. He came to a sliding stop and hopped off. Instead of him getting in, I met him at the tailgate of the pickup. I dropped the gate with a creaking thud. It may have knocked some rust off when it fell. I hopped up and spun around and plopped down on the gate. The suspension sank as I rested on the gate. Timmy tried to sit next to me. I stopped him and told him to stand on the road. He backed up and kicked some rocks out from under his feet.

"What do you know today, Timmy?" I asked, knowing that he had been in contact with Chris.

"Well, I think Chris has a shipment coming in this week, cuz he called me yesterday."

"Okay. So, let's get this going. I need you to tell me everything you know about Chris."

"Well, like I said, he gets his shit from this Asian stripper. She's a stripper at the 'Blew Bayou' in Hastings."

"What's his connection with this Asian stripper, as you put it, aside from her supplying him with meth and weed?"

"I ain't sure."

"Okay, what's her name?"

"Joy."

"Of course, it is," I responded, knowing that it's her stage name.

"I think it really is Joy." He emphasized "really."

"Have you met her?"

"Ya, she's fucking hot!" he said, adjusting his crotch.

I put my head down and shook it in disgust. I hate going to strip clubs, contrary to what people think. They are dirty and a lot of shady shit goes on in there. This particular strip club is owned by a member of the Sons of Violence Motorcycle Club in Hastings. He allegedly won it in a poker game years ago. How true that is? I don't know, but it's what I heard.

"All right, let's buy some dope from Chris," I said energetically, slapping the gate of the truck. More rust shavings fell to the ground.

Timmy looked at me, then my truck, and said under his breath, "What a piece of shit."

"Well, we could ride tandem on yer bike."

Timmy gave a sarcastic chuckle.

"Today's Tuesday, let's buy from Chris on Friday after he's off work at three. Can you call him and set it up?"

"Yep, no problem. How much ya want me to buy?"

"How much you normally buy from him?"

Timmy thought about it for a second, "A gram."

"That's it? Let's try for more."

"I can get a ball from him, I bet."

"Good, we'll do that. Meet here at noon on Friday."

"You got it, boss."

Timmy jumped back on his bike and scurried off toward the blacktop like he was shot in the ass with a pellet gun. I needed to go do some homework on Chris and Joy. I wish I had a partner to help with this shit, it really would make things easier.

I gathered all my equipment and gear for a stakeout on Thursday night so I wouldn't be rummaging around the day of trying to find everything. When doing a stakeout by yourself, it is important to make sure you have security measures in plan.

The plan starts with the right vehicle. In *Miami Vice*, a white Ferrari Testarossa was used. In *Magnum PI*, a bright red Ferrari 308GT. These are not good vehicles to use for a couple different reasons. One, too flashy. Even for Miami or Hawaii, these cars will stick out. And two, lack of security. It is too easy for someone to sneak up on you. A low vehicle with only two seats is not practical. I understand they are only television shows, but a lot of people equate TV with real life.

I used a silver minivan for my stakeouts. Silver minivans are one of the most popular vehicles in middle Iowa, aside from pickups. However, minivans are very functional, and they blend in. The little old lady that gets up to pee at two in the morning is not going to think anything of the minivan parked in the street. But a big black Suburban or Tahoe, that will raise some concerns, and she will call the department you are employed at, for a suspicious vehicle parked on her block. It really sucks to have an operation blown due to your ego.

In a minivan, there is a lot of room to move around to be comfortable. Nothing worse than doing a ten-hour stakeout in cramped quarters. Except, making the fatal mistake of eating a convenience store burrito while doing that ten-hour stakeout. I would remove the back seats and use a folding lawn chair to sit in. Believe it or not, they are very comfortable but not too comfortable that you fall asleep. Sleeping is not recommended on stakeouts.

Some of the other things I would make sure to have during a long operation are bottles of water and one empty Gatorade bottle, the thirty-two-ounce kind, for obvious reasons. Yes, I have peed in a plastic bottle in a vehicle numerous times. When you gotta go, you gotta go.

Weapons, you must have weapons. I had my trusty Glock 23 with at least four extra mags and a tac light. I would also keep my AR along my side. There's a comfort level with an AR that makes me feel all warm and fuzzy. And of course, extra mags for it as well.

In my "go bag," a SOG SEAL Pup five-inch fixed blade knife. This is a very dependable knife that is also functional and durable. The blade is half-beveled edge and half-serrated, and very sharp. I carry an SOG Flash assisted opening folding knife with a three-and half-inch blade in my right pocket for quick use.

Extra batteries also made home in my "go bag." AA, AAA, CR123, all had a use for the equipment I carried. Two extra flashlights, a Surefire Stinger, and a Surefire weapon-mounted tac light. In the event I needed to replace the batteries or bulb of my tac light, I could remove it and replace it with a functioning one. My body mic recording device for the CI. Camcorder with low light capabilities, a digital camera, and night vision goggles. My chief was able to hook me up from the military DRMO (Defense Reutilization Marketing Office), which is a Department of Defense company that sells refurbished military items to civilians and other military branches.

Other items I made sure to have were my cell phone and charger, a pad of paper with multiple pens and pencils, a reading magazine, a police radio, my police badge, two sets of handcuffs and key, and body armor, always bring your vest. And snacks, you need to have snacks.

Prior to the operation, I would conduct reconnaissance missions to evaluate and assess the area. This is important to know your background—where to park, where are the best areas to watch from, the avenues of escape, what street lights are operational and which ones are not, how many vehicles are on the street or in the parking lot, where do people take their breaks, what time the shifts start and end, how many employees, and when is sunset or sunrise. I equate this as scouting a baseball player. All the information is there, you just need to find it and apply it.

This recon mission usually takes anywhere from two days to two weeks, depending on what exactly the mission is. Since this mission is utilizing a CI, we will need to meet at a predetermined location. Timmy is my CI, so we will be meeting at the cemetery and then traveling to the garage of city hall to pat him down and do a briefing of the night's upcoming events.

All I needed to do was grab my buy money from the chief, and I would be good to go. I met with Chief Walters at the police department. He doesn't stray from the PD during his shift, unless called out. He handed me an envelope with three hundred dollars in $20, $10, and $5 along with a currency log form. We made small talk while I logged and photographed each bill. Once I was done, I stashed it in my chain wallet. At least this way, I know I won't lose it. A loose envelope is more likely to be misplaced.

I briefly explained to the chief of the operation I was about to conduct on Chris—info about the factory he works for and his role at the company. Also, the Asian stripper, which he was more interested in than anything. It may have had something to do with him being in Vietnam, but I'm not sure.

He knew these operations could take days and long hours. I explained to him how there would be three controlled buys on Chris, then get him to roll on his supplier, the stripper, Joy. I also told him this could produce more local arrests as he is the primary supplier at West Star Co. He questioned how many, maybe five, ten or twenty people. He told me he would like to get that place shut down because of the drug trafficking. He told me a folklore of the factory being a drug distribution center in the 1970s and a song made about it. I have yet to hear the song, but I can about imagine how it would go.

CHAPTER 23

I did not sleep well, going over all the problematic situations that Murphy's law is going to send at me. "If it can go wrong, it will." I must clear my head of the negatives and focus on the positives. This is a good operation; I've done my homework. I have as much information and intelligence on the factory, building, employees, my target, and my CI as I can. What can go wrong?

Friday, 1230 hours: Timmy had not shown up yet. We were supposed to meet at noon at the cemetery. Here I sat in my silver minivan, becoming more and more anxious. *This little shit stood me up*, I thought to myself as I scanned the cemetery and out to the edge of town trying to locate him.

Now 1300 hours, I saw a person on a bike riding toward me on a city street. The rider cut across a vacant lot and still traveling toward me. As he got to the blacktop, I saw that it was Timmy on yet a different BMX bike.

As he got closer, I stepped out of the van to get some fresh air in my lungs and clear my head before I say a word to Timmy. He conducted his signature powerslide and dropped the bike all in one motion.

"What's up, boss? Ya ready to do this?" he asked enthusiastically.

"Where the fuck you been, Timmy? It's after one," I questioned as I stepped forward into his personal space.

He leaned back and took a step back with bugging out eyes and mouth agape. He put both hands to indicate separation of us.

"Wait, huh?" he responded, clearly confused.

"What time did I tell you to be here?"

"One. You said one!"

"No, you little tweaker, I said noon!"

"Shit, my bad."

"When I give you a time to be somewhere, you be there. You got it?"

"Yep, won't happen again, I promise," he replied as he crossed his heart with his left hand on the right side of his chest.

"Wrong side, dumbass."

"Huh?"

"Never mind. Let's go, get in the van." I ordered as I turned and got into the driver's side.

Timmy jumped in the passenger side sliding door and sat on the floor. I wanted him in the back because the windows were tinted, and you can't see in as we drive through town to city hall. I don't want anyone to see him.

When we arrived, I opened the garage with the garage door opener and waited until it was clear for me to move forward. As soon as I entered, I hit the button again and waited until the door was all the way down before we exited the van.

"Come on." I told Timmy.

We entered the building and walked to my office. The building was quiet as it is a holiday for the employees, except for me, I get to work on holidays. Once we got into my office, I shut the door behind Timmy and told him to empty out all of his pockets. He seemed confused. I told him again.

"Why?"

"Because I don't want you getting anything for yourself. I need to make sure you don't have any money or weapons or pipes or product on you."

"Fine," he said reluctantly.

As a narcotics officer, there are quite a few tactics and practices used and passed along that prove to be beneficial. One important practice when working with informants is to search them before and after a controlled buy. This is to eliminate any personal gains the informant may have in mind, such as purchasing contraband for personal use at a later time. All money, weapons, and paraphernalia are confiscated, as well as drugs. Not too often does this happen, but I have encountered it, such as this time.

As Timmy emptied out his pockets and placed the contents on my desk, I saw that he had almost the exact same stuff as he did when I first busted him the night we met.

"There, that's it," he said, holding up his hands like a cowboy roping a calf for time.

I inspected the Marlboro Menthol pack of cigarettes and the lighters, the cell phone and wadded-up papers.

"Where is it?"

"Where is what?"

"The meth, where is it?"

"Man, I don't have any shit on me! I'm serious!" Timmy pleaded.

I slammed my fist on the desk causing a boisterous thud. This scared Timmy to point he jumped back and fell over the gray metal chair.

"Okay! Fuck, dude! You need to chill!" he said as he helped himself up from the floor.

I stood there staring at him, my right hand throbbing and my face becoming red with a drop of sweat forming on my forehead. Timmy stared at me and then gave a sigh of exhaustion.

"Fine," he said as he bent over and lifted his right pant leg, then reached into the cuff of his sock and retrieved a clear plastic baggie with meth in it.

He gently placed it on the desk with his other items as if it were a Robin's egg.

I picked it up and examined it, it was about a half of gram. Pretty good meth, judging from the color, clearly not "Anny Dope."

"Where did you get this?" I interrogated Timmy.

"I dunno, a friend, I guess."

"Did you get it from Chris?"

"No, I told him I would be meeting with him today. I didn't want to mess that up." He reasoned.

"Fine, we will be dealing with this later," I said as I walked to the evidence locker and opened it. I took a small light brown paper bag from the locker and wrote: "Do not touch. PDQ," in Sharpie. Then shut and locked the locker.

I took out my body mic recording wire from its protective black Pelican case to attach to Timmy. He was very apprehensive about wearing a mic. I told him there is no way he was doing it without wearing one, especially now.

As a contingency plan, he will also have his phone on and muted while talking with Chris.

Timmy cannot be trusted, and this is about the only way I feel comfortable doing this. I ran the wire on the inside of his brown leather belt. This is typically a good place to hide it because it is too close to his crotch and makes people uncomfortable to search there. Usually, the wire is placed on the person's chest and is the first place looked.

Once we got it situated, we went back out to the minivan. Again, he lay down in the back as I exited the garage and reunited him with "his" BMX bike at the cemetery.

I dropped him off at his bike and asked him if he had any questions. I think we went over everything well. He told me he would meet Chris at his car in the parking lot of West Star Company. I had already reconned the area and told him where it was parked. I would be close by watching and waiting. I did not want Timmy to know exactly where I would be parked because he would incessantly glance over at the van. It is human nature in a high-stress situation to be concerned where the comfort is coming from. He unconsciously would be looking for me.

Timmy will need to ride his bike from across town to the manufacturing plant. I would wait for him in the area and provide cover. Also, the mic has very limited range, about one thousand unobstructed feet to be exact. By Timmy riding his bike, it would appear that he came from his apartment as it is on the opposite side of town, and Chris knows that.

Timmy arrived in the West Star Company parking lot and began to the search for Chris's car. Chris is a large fella, about six foot two and 325 pounds. He smokes two packs of Camels a day and eats a bag of Doritos for lunch. Needless to say, physical fitness is not of importance to him. Chris is the type of guy who will arrive to work early so he can get a close parking spot, so he doesn't have to walk across the parking lot.

Timmy entered from the blacktop entrance and located Chris's black 1995 Pontiac Grand Prix in the third row. From my vantage point, I have a bird's eye view of his car. Across the street is Kelley's Auto Mart. He sells "quality" used cars at a "discounted" price. It sits on a hill and overlooks the parking lot of the factory. I know Mr. Kelley and use his vehicles for surveillance and other undercover operations.

So, naturally, I asked him to move a vehicle so I could park the van there. I explained to him that I am waiting for a warrant suspect to get off work and didn't want him to get spooked by a squad car. He offered me a soda and asked if he could help. I told him not on this one, but the next one he sure could.

One advantage about parking here is, I can turn on the air-conditioning. Usually at night in residential areas, I can't turn on the AC or the heat because I can't have the vehicle running. It draws too much attention. Sitting in my lawn chair with the binos lying on my lap, I turned on my handheld police radio and placed it next to me on the floor. I tucked my badge into my shirt and adjusted the volume on the body mic receiver.

Timmy was sitting on Chris's Pontiac hood waiting impatiently, smoking a menthol cigarette. Approximately ten minutes went by when I saw Chris walking out of the factory primary doors. He was talking with a man in his fifties and shook hands; they went their separate ways. Chris spotted Timmy and put his hand up and waved. Timmy waved back like they were long lost brothers meeting at an airport terminal. He slid off the hood and waited patiently for Chris to make his way through the maze of parked cars.

"What's up buddy?" Chris asked, overly excited.

"Nada, brah! Just waiting for you!"

"What ya need today?" Chris asked.

"A ball," Timmy responded.

The mic was coming in clearer today than any other day I used it. Maybe because on my elevated position, maybe a crystal-clear day, maybe…maybe… Murphy's law, and it is setting me up for failure.

"A ball?" Chris questioned emphatically.

"Yep, a ball."

"Timmy, I know you got busted a while back. Ya better not be settin' me up, brah," Chris replied with an authoritative voice.

"Settin' you up? Hell na, brah! I wouldn't do that! Yer my boy!" Timmy stated as he fidgeted in his pocket, pleading for the trust of Chris.

I could hear the tone of Timmy's voice go from fun and energetic to nervous and anxious. This worried me. *Don't lose your shit, Timmy,* I thought to myself.

"A ball, huh." Chris looked at Timmy, trying to see some indication of distrust or malice. He contemplated for a moment, then smiled.

"Here, check this out," Chris said as he dropped his backpack on the factory's concrete and moved to the rear of his car.

He pushed a button on his key fob, and the trunk popped open, then assisted it open to extension. Chris bent over and opened a black duffle bag about two feet by two feet. Inside the bag were two kilos of meth and multiple handguns with magazines and loose ammunition. Timmy stepped back in amazement and put his hands behind his head in the surrender cobra position.

"Holy fuck, dude! Where the fuck did you get that?" Timmy yelled.

"Keep yer voice down, dude! Jesus Christ! Ya wanna get busted? This shit ain't all mine, I gotta deliver it today." Chris said as he turned around and pushed Timmy with his left hand.

"Sorry, dude, I ain't ever seen that much white."

Whoa, wait, what the hell is he looking at? I can't see inside the trunk. I hope Timmy is smart enough to say the amount out loud. I begged internally for Timmy to come through for me, how much is there? I tried getting a better angle with the binos and adjusted the focus, hoping I could see in the trunk. No luck. All I could see was their upper bodies.

"Two keys? Man, dude, yer movin' up in the world," Timmy said to Chris, slapping him on his back.

I spit my water all over the inside of the rear window. Did he just say two keys? Holy shit!

Two kilos of meth in the trunk of the car sitting there all day. What the hell is wrong with this guy? I'm going to hook this guy up today, no way am I letting two kilos of meth out on the street, not in my town.

"Hell, ya! Wanna see something even cooler?" Chris asked in his best television criminal voice with a smirk.

"Sure!" Timmy said like a child on his birthday asking for the next present.

Chris moved the duffle bag to the side and lifted the spare tire cover up so they could see in there.

"Here, hold this up," Chris asked Timmy to help.

Timmy held the cover up while Chris reached down and pulled out an identical duffle bag with the same dimensions. Timmy set the cover down in its place. Chris placed the bag down on the cover and unzipped it. Inside was the most money Timmy had ever seen in his life. Forty thousand dollars in stacks of one thousand dollars in one-hundred-dollar bills with rubber bands around them.

"I already sold two keys, dude. There's forty thou, right there," Chris said with an accomplished smile on his face.

I spit my water all over the inside of the back window again. Forty thousand dollars? Two kilos of meth and forty thousand dollars! The mother lode!

I called my friend Adam, a deputy for the local county sheriff.

"Adam! Adam!" I anxiously exclaimed.

"Calm down, what's going on?" he asked, confused with my excitement.

"Drop whatever the fuck yer doin'. You need to grab yer gear and get to Kelley's Auto now. I'm about to make the biggest bust of the county!" I said in one breath.

"Okay, I'll be there in two minutes," he responded.

Adam knows me well and knows if I am that excited, something serious is about to go down.

While waiting for Adam, Chris sold Timmy an eight ball of the same quality of meth that's in the duffle bag in the truck. Not that I needed the individual sale, but it did help for the distribution case.

Less than two minutes, Adam showed up and pulled in behind my minivan. He jogged to the passenger side and opened the door. I didn't move anything for him. He pushed all the paper, radio, and other equipment to the floor and sat down.

"What the fuck is going on?" he asked, still confused.

"Two keys of meth and forty thousand dollars."

"What?"

"Yep."

"Who is it?"

I explained the whole story to Adam as we sat there waiting for Timmy and Chris to finish their deal. As I was explaining this to Adam, Chris shut the trunk lid and got into the driver's side with Timmy following by getting in the passenger seat. The car backed out of the parking space and made its way to the exit of the factory parking lot.

I crawled into the driver's seat and put the van in drive. I handed him the binos and asked Adam to watch where Chris's car was going as I drive. It turned toward us on the blacktop and crossed the highway. As it passed us, I saw Timmy looking at us with a concerned expression, and Chris was looking at Timmy. I pulled in behind the car after it had passed us and followed it for a few miles out of town. The Pontiac approached a gravel road north of town and turned east onto the road. The car came to a stop about a quarter mile off the blacktop.

I stopped the van and made a three-point turn in the middle of the blacktop to turn around, step on the accelerator, and turn east on the gravel road. As we approached the stationary car, the driver's side door opened and there Chris stood with a pistol pointed at the van. I slammed on the brakes and threw it in park. Adam and I threw our doors open, exited the car in a tactical maneuver, and drew our weapons.

"Drop the gun! Police! Drop the gun!" I shouted at Chris. "Drop it, mother fucker!"

Chris dropped the gun on the gravel road and stepped to the side while throwing his hands high in the air like a referee signaling a touchdown. I approached Chris while Adam walked toward the passenger side. Adam knew Timmy was my CI but treated him like a suspect to continue the charade, so Chris didn't get suspicious.

"Lemme see yer hands!" Adam ordered Timmy.

Timmy followed the command and stuck his arms out the window.

"Open the door with your left hand and step out! Do it now!" Adam shouted with his Sig P226 pointed at him.

Timmy complied and stepped out facing away from Adam. He immediately put his hands above his head and awaited his next series of commands. Timmy has been in this situation before and knew the drill all too well.

"Step back to me!" Adam continued with the commands. "Stop! Now on the ground, get on the ground!"

Timmy reluctantly submitted to the orders and lied down on his stomach on the gravel road, feeling the pebbles dig into his skin.

Adam checked my status with Chris. I holstered my weapon and proceeded to handcuff Chris while he lied on his front side. I patted down Chris and found a full fifteen-round magazine for his 9mm Hi Point Model C-9 pistol tucked in his belt. A Hi Point pistol is a common gun for dopers because of their availability and price. They are about 150 dollars from a gun store and about fifty dollars when buying a stolen one.

I couldn't wait to see all the goodies in the trunk of this piece of shit. I helped Chris get propped up on the driver's side rear tire. After I located the keys in the ignition, I unlocked the trunk. Adam had drug Timmy to the opposite tire from Chris. I held the trunk lid from opening until Adam had his total attention on the trunk and its contents.

"Ready?"

Adam nodded his head in approval.

I lifted the trunk lid and there before us on this dusty gravel road surrounded by natures cover of cornfields were two black duffle bags with what was going to make us famous and hated. Two evenly weighted kilos of methamphetamine, multiple handguns, magazines, and ammunition in one duffle and the other duffle bag containing forty thousand dollars in crisp, new, one-hundred-dollar bills.

"Oooweee!" Adam shouted as he leaned back in amazement. "I ain't ever seen that much money!"

"Who is on duty right now for you guys?" I asked Adam.

"Deputy Peterson."

"Cool, call him up here and get this car towed to the PD. I need to debrief these assholes immediately."

"I ain't sayin' shit!" Chris chimed in.

"Ya, we'll see," I replied.

Adam called Deputy Peterson and requested him to come to our location, and he would explain everything then. I assisted Chris to his feet and walked him to the minivan. The seats had all been removed so Chris and Timmy will have to ride back sitting on the floor of the van. Adam picked Timmy up with one motion and walked him to the van and ordered him in. Timmy mumbled something about Adam's mother, so Timmy got a friendly reminder of his role.

Once Deputy Peterson arrived, we briefly explained the scenario and asked that he get the car impounded and towed to my department. I removed the evidence from the trunk and set it in front with me so there is no break in the chain of custody. We removed ourselves from the scene and drove to the sheriff department's jail. Now the fun begins.

CHAPTER 24

With Chris in one interview room and Timmy in the other, Adam and I corroborated our tactics. We need to obtain as much information from Chris as possible. This may be tougher than expected. However, Chris is looking at a lot of felony charges including:

- Possession with the Intent to Deliver Methamphetamine (Iowa Code Sec. 124.401; a Class B felony),
- Failure to Affix Drug Tax Stamp (Iowa Code Sec. 453B; a Class D Felony), and
- Felon in Possession of a Firearm times five (Iowa Code Sec. 124.26; a Class D Felony).

And some misdemeanor charges as well:

- Carrying a Firearm without a Permit (Iowa Code Sec. 724.4; an Aggravated Misdemeanor),
- Driving Without a License (Iowa Code Sec. 321.274), and
- No Insurance (Iowa Code Sec. 321.55).

I entered the interview room where Timmy was. The room was only twelve feet by twelve feet and had dark gray corrugated foam attached to the cinder block walls to help with the acoustics. A lone wooden table with silver metal legs sat in the center of the room with a blue plastic chair for the suspect and a black soft padded chair on rollers for the interviewer. He was sitting in the chair with his head resting on his crossed arms on the table.

"Timmy!" I shouted and got his attention.

"What?" he responded as he lifted his head.

"So, what can you tell me about where he got the meth and where the rest is going?"

"All I know is it's going to the twins up in Hastings and he got it from Joy."

"Mikey and Jeremy, right?"

"Yep."

What's Joy's last name?"

"I don't know."

"Which town does she live in? Hastings?"

"Ya, Hastings. It's a nice house on a dead-end street."

Timmy looked up to the ceiling and squinted like he was holding in a fart. He adjusted in his seat and began to form some shapes with his mouth as if he is sounding out words until they sound right.

"Great! Thanks, Timmy! Okay, so here's the deal. I need you to stay in the jail tonight."

His smile went to a scowl. "Fuck that! I helped you, why would I need to stay in jail?"

"I need ya to get more information from Chris. If I let you go tonight, what will he think? So, tomorrow mornin', yer 'Gramma' will bail you out, and tonight you will get as much information as you can. The cell will be bugged, Adam and I will be listening. Cool?"

He agreed and realized he didn't have anywhere else to be anyway. I escorted him to his cell; at which time, he gave me a hearty "fuck you" loud enough that other inmates including Chris could hear him. The steel-barred cell door slammed shut behind him with a thunderous *bang*!

Adam and I entered the interview room, which Chris occupied. The room mimicked the interview room Timmy was in. I gently laid my black leather legal-size notepad down on the table and situated my chair, so I was directly across from Chris. Adam moved his hard, blue plastic chair to the right of Chris. This would better help us read his body language and gauge his temperament.

I opened the notebook and found a clean piece of paper and began writing notes. Chris was watching intently and every so often glanced over to Adam.

"Chris, my name is Phil Quick. I am the narcotics investigator for the area task force, and I am here to discuss your future. Before I ask you any questions, I need to read something to you, do you understand?" I began as I normally do during a narcotics debriefing.

"Whatever, dude."

"Good."

I removed a yellow laminated card the size of a playing card from my notebook. I got this card at DEA school and have had ever since and used it quite frequently. I use only this card when I read someone their Miranda Rights so when I testify, I can bring the card with me and show the court that I read this card and this card only verbatim. So, there is not a question about what I said or if I forgot to mention a portion of the Rights to the suspect. I cleared my throat and began.

"Chris, I'm going to be asking you questions about the crimes that you may or may not have committed. In order for me to do that, I need to read you something. Do you understand?" I formally spoke to Chris as serious as I could.

"Go fuck yourself," was his eloquent response.

"I'm going to need a yes or no."

Chris looked down in disappointment that he didn't get the response he was looking for. Unfortunately for him, this was not my first rodeo. I knew the games and could play them well.

"I'm going to read you a series of statements. After I read each statement, I'll ask you if you understand. If you reply with yes, I'll continue. If you reply with a no, I will explain the statement that I just read before moving on to the next one. Do you understand?"

Chris nodded his head.

"I need a verbal yes or no." I reiterated.

"Yes," he finally said reluctantly and mockingly.

"Okay. Let's begin. You have the right to remain silent. Do you understand that?"

"Yes."

"Anything you say can be used in court. Do you understand?"

"Ya."

"You have the right to talk to a lawyer for advice before we ask you any questions and to have a lawyer with you during questioning. Do you understand that?"

Chris nodded his head. I paused and waited for a verbal confirmation. He looked up at me.

"Yes," Chris said crisply.

"Good. If you cannot afford a lawyer, one will be appointed for you before any questioning if you wish. Do you understand?"

"Yes," he said sarcastically.

"Are you willing to answer some questions that we have?" I finally asked.

Chris shrugged his shoulders as to question. He looked away and down while folding his hands in his lap. This is typically a sign of closure for a person being questioned.

The entire interview lasted for two hours. There was a lot of back and forth, cat and mouse. But in the end, Chris realized that the only way he was going to be able to help himself is to comply with the inevitable that I will not give up.

Chris relinquished information regarding the location of the future drop for the two kilos of meth and where he was to take the money. A motivated person such as Chris is an easier target than someone who has nothing to lose. Chris was looking at being a three-strike felon and possible federal prison time. I explained to Chris how I could and would help him by not calling the ATF or the DEA, and he could help himself and me with this investigation. He questioned how that would help him. I explained it like this:

As someone who was arrested for possession with the intent to deliver two kilos of methamphetamine and five handguns with ammunition plus the forty thousand dollars that shows his involvement with the active drug trafficking and can be prosecuted in the Federal Court system where he would have to serve 85 percent of his sentence. Also, him being a three-strike felon, it would be life without parole under the Violent Crime Control and Law Enforcement Act of 1994, which includes drug trafficking and weapon possession. He could possibly be indicted under the RICO Act (Racketeer Influenced and Corrupt Organization Act) along with all the other people he had ties with regarding the drug trafficking. Now, the RICO Act would be a stretch, but he didn't know that.

At twenty-seven years old and looking at spending the rest of his life in a federal prison is a fantastic reason to be a motivated "cooperant" with law enforcement. Chris signed his name on the dotted line to assist us and now worked for us as an informant. However, he will be doing a minimum of three controlled buys for each charge, which means I will be spending a lot of time with Chris. Up to bat is Joy.

Timmy was released of his obligation to be a confidential informant. He was able to produce more than expected and quite honestly, I think I might miss the little shit. By the time we were complete with the operation that Timmy assisted with, there were seven indictments. He was not required to testify, and I was able to secure his identity. The only people who knew he helped us were the law enforcements officers involved and anyone he told.

For someone like Timmy to be dedicated enough to do this, he had to have significant motivation. Not seeing his new child was that motivation. Timmy moved from Iowa with his family to a southern state. He received a clean record; I hope he stays clean. Good luck, Timmy.

CHAPTER 25

Joy Nyguen is a thirty-six-year-old Laotian woman who not only is a stripper at the Blew Bayou gentlemen's club in Hastings, but she is also the manager. She resides by herself in a small one-story house in Hastings, Iowa. Joy is five feet, two inches tall and about 105 pounds. She has long black hair with light-colored highlights and usually keeps it down. She dresses as if she is living in California and not the Midwest. She drives a white 2000 BMW 750i with low profile wheels. Joy is also educated and has a business degree from Cal State Fresno.

She is considered high maintenance, but it's really not much trouble to keep this attractive when she is naturally. Joy is a beautiful woman, but her attitude overshadows her beauty. To put it mildly, Joy is not a nice lady. I think there is a name for it, but I don't recall.

Joy has ties to central California, where she is originally from. This brings up the explanation of where she gets her large quantities of methamphetamine. She is rumored to receive loads of cocaine as well, but this had not been confirmed yet. She has people working for her who delivers the drugs. Instead of using planes or buses, her people drive the drugs cross-country. It is easier to get through all the security measures put in place after 9/11. Yes, there are a lot of ways to get stopped by law enforcement on the highways, but if you obey the speed limits and don't make yourself conspicuous, then you'll get to your destination without a hitch.

According to Chris, Joy has a shipment of white that arrives to her every other Thursday. There are four different routes that are used. Every shipment uses a different route, and the route is not known until the day of the delivery. This helps eliminate both law enforcement and pirates. Yes, I said pirates. Not the ones on the Caribbean high seas but the ones who operate the same way, only on the highways. But the pirates leave dead bodies as well as stolen merchandise.

Joy's crew also use different cars that they get from rental companies. They register in different names and use various companies. This breaks up the rhythm and keeps people guessing. She has a platoon of people she uses, primarily women because they are less suspicious. When the women arrive, Joy has them work in the club for a week and then they return to California. The women are on a specific rotation where they won't come back until after six months. It's a very detailed and efficient process.

The product is then distributed throughout the Midwest. Hastings is used because it is a small enough town that law enforcement is oblivious and untrained of the west coast drug trafficking methods. But it's large enough that the strip club clientele can blend in with the other businesses and locals.

She uses the mobility of the outlaw motorcycle club, the Sons of Violence MC. They have chapters all over the United States and have the access to travel without being harassed. Outlaw motorcycle gangs have been at war with law enforcement for many, many years. The evolution of the battle has transpired to now with the use of drones and tier 3 wire taps from the occasional traffic stop and use of undercover operations. Technology has changed the playing field. The one thing that has not changed is the law and outlaws.

The bikers, along with their mobility and ease of movement throughout the US, hang with the type of people who consume and buy controlled substances. This makes them an essential player in the game of drug trafficking. With the lifestyle of swap meets, rallies, parties, get-togethers, and so on, they are constantly around large groups of people in their same line of "work." And if you want to see something funny, watching a five-foot-nothing, hundred-pound-nothing woman yelling and striking fear in a big bad biker is quite entertaining.

Chris is going to introduce me to Joy as his cousin from Des Moines. I continue to use Des Moines because it's a large enough city that running into someone from there would be improbable. My back story is the same as it usually is to help keep things consistent and easy to remember. I'm originally from Muscatine, Iowa, and moved to Des Moines a few years ago after serving time in the brig when I was arrested for selling cocaine while in the Marine Corps. My area of expertise is cutting meth and cocaine, then selling it.

I use a product for cutting called MSM or the chemical term, methylsulfonylmethane. MSM is a clear crystalline powder that mixes nicely with crystal meth and has no side effects or odd tastes. But let's be honest, if you're putting meth in your body, I'm sure you're not concerned with the taste.

I can turn one pound of 90 percent meth into three pounds of 50 percent meth. To put that in monetary terms, a kilo of crystal meth is 2.2 pounds and valued at twenty-five thousand dollars. Once I'm done with it, is now six pounds of meth, but at a lower consistency at seventy-five thousand dollars. Also, when selling individual use, I will be selling it, overall, at a higher rate than if one were to buy a kilo up front. Hence the term "druganomics." This type of logic is something a drug trafficker and businesswoman can understand. Oh, the power of money.

CHAPTER 26

After the interview with Chris, we decided on a time and place to meet working around his work schedule. This was important because there are a lot of people who buy drugs from Chris at West Star Company, and I don't want anyone to get suspicious. Chris and Timmy will be working for me without each other knowing it. However, Timmy will know that I'm working Chris but not the other way around.

I met with Chris at the same spot in the cemetery but quickly realized it would not work well. Chris's car stood out, not like Timmy on his bike. I needed to find a new location. I called one of my deputy friends and asked if I could use their sally port. He said yes, but the problem with this location is the time frame. We will have to meet after dark when the courthouse and jail staff are gone for the day.

I texted Chris and told him to meet me at the sheriff's office back parking lot and wait for my instructions. This Friday evening, Chris is going to introduce me to Joy at the Blew Bayou. I haven't been to a strip club since my days in the Marine Corps. This will be interesting.

I arrived about thirty minutes prior to Chris and texted him to come to the sally port and parked his car concealed. Once he shut the ignition off, before we went any further, I had him empty out his pockets and then patted him down. I did not trust this guy at all. It probably won't

233

be as fun as it is working with Timmy. Maybe that guy is growing on me, I don't know.

"Empty yer pockets, Chris." I instructed him.

"Why do I need to do all this, man? This is dumb," he responded.

"Look, you do what I say when I say it. Any variation of that, you go to jail without hesitation or remorse. Ya get it?" I sternly said.

Yeah, it was kind of a show of dominance with him, but I needed to establish these rules. Informants are like children; they push the envelope to see how far they can go. I am putting up barriers, so he doesn't push too far. Unfortunately, I do need Chris for the introduction, which sucks, I don't like this guy, but it is what it is.

"Now put yer hands up and turn around. I'm going to pat you down. Do you have anything on you that I need to be aware of?" I ordered.

"Na, man. I got nothin'."

"Good, this will be easy then."

"This is going to suck," he said under his breath.

"Uh, huh."

Once I was finished patting Chris down, we took the elevator to the third floor of the sheriff's office to a meeting room that I had set up for the debriefing. Adam escorted us through the sheriff's office and unlocked the door.

"After you," he said as he held out his hand like a waiter sitting us down at a table in a fancy restaurant.

"Gracias, amigo," I replied in my best Spanish.

"Sit down there." I told Chris as I pointed to the empty plastic chair across the table from the other two chairs.

I placed two nice comfortable office chairs on one side of the table and a hard plastic chair on the other side for Chris. This is done on purpose to make Chris uncomfortable, so he doesn't get too relaxed that he forgets the task at hand.

"So here's the plan. You are going to introduce me to Joy as your cousin, like we discussed earlier. Do you remember where I'm from?" I asked.

"Ya, Des Moines."

"Good, yer payin' attention. I need you to really sell the fact that I am here to buy as much white as I can get. She needs to believe that I am a dealer in an outlaw biker club, and I have a lot of friends and connections in low places. Do you understand?"

"Ya, I can do that."

"Adam, yer goin' to be my cover and be listening in, right?"

"Yes, sir," he answered in a military manner.

"Good. We'll head that way about twenty hundred hours. There's an L-shaped parking lot there. I'll park on the north side closest to the road. Since we are in a residential area, you park down the street and blend in with the locals. The music's goin' to be loud, you'll have a hard time hearing what we're saying, but do what you can. Cool?" I instructed as I got out the paperwork to finish before we left.

There is so much paperwork when doing these operations. It is very tedious but needs to be done. I hate looking stupid on the stand when testifying. I don't like the defense attorneys to have any loopholes for their clients when I go

235

to court. This stuff is difficult enough as it is without those jackasses making it harder.

I asked Adam to stay with Chris while I get ready in his office. I don't want Chris to see me putting together my undercover "uniform" because if things go sideways and he turns, he will know where I keep my hidden weapons and mic. That could be bad for me, if you know what I mean.

I put my vest on over my black sleeveless T-shirt. "Support your local PRMC" written in silver on the front and "Behold I saw a Pale Horse, it's rider named death and hell followed" in the same lettering on the back. I had these T-shirts specially made along with stickers, patches, and a hat.

I checked the integrated sheath for my palm knife and my secret pocket for the handcuff key. I inserted the mic wire through the seams and left some slack for the plug in. I'm not wearing a bandana, but I have it in my back left pocket with a little special surprise. I put a two-ounce steel ball bearing in the bandana and tied it off with a piece of leather. If I need to, I can pull it out of my pocket by the tail and swing it around, then bonk someone on the head. It's an old biker trick, it's not a weapon but can be used as one if needed.

I checked my backup pistol in my left boot. I carried a snub nose Taurus .357, silver and black, in the inside of my left boot. It is a little uncomfortable, but two is one. I also only have five rounds in the cylinder. The first round is chambered so that the hammer falls on an empty chamber. This way, if someone gets it away from me and pulls the trigger, it goes "click" and not "boom." Some will say this is not a good tactic, but after a lengthy conversation with an old undercover narc from Texas, this is how I now carry it. Plus, I know it will fall on an empty chamber, so I'm prepared for it.

I removed the Glock from my lower back position and ejected the magazine. Thirteen rounds, checked. I inserted the mag and replaced the Glock in my waistband and adjusted it to be comfortable. I gave myself a quick once-over and took a big deep inhale and released slowly. Here we go!

I returned to the interview room and knocked on the door. It opened, and Chris was seated in his chair with his head down in his crossed arms on the table. Adam smiled at me with that look, like we are about to get in a bar fight.

"Chris! Wake up!" I shouted.

"Jesus Christ! I'm awake!"

Adam and I were laughing, and fist-bumped each other. I have now transformed into this ruthless biker whom no one wants to fuck with.

CHAPTER 27

We pulled into the city limits of Hastings; Chris and I in my undercover Ford pickup that he complained about for the whole trip. Adam in his cover vehicle, a 2000 gray Chevrolet Tahoe LT. Black and dark blue Tahoes look like police vehicles, but the gray fits in with the locals. Before we met with Chris, we set up the Tahoe with all our backup equipment. The way undercover operations on TV and in the movies are so fake. It is never shown how much shit goes into the operation itself, not just the buy but also the preparation and intel.

I slowed down as I approached the parking lot. There were five or so Harleys parked at an angle and front wheel to the street in front of the bars entrance. Approximately ten cars parked sporadically in the parking lot. I pulled into the lot and drove around the building to the back. I did this to see if there were any surprises waiting for us. I found a parking spot on the north side of the building and backed my truck into the spot between two cars. I reiterated to Chris the importance of this evening and how it could make him or break him. He nodded in acknowledgment.

I conducted a comm check with Adam.

"Lima Charlie," he responded.

The music was thumping and was audible enough that I could tell what song was playing. The neighbors have to love this! As we walked across the rock and broken pavement parking lot, the music got louder when a patron opened the door to step out for fresh air. I scanned the area and noticed the bouncer watching us walking toward him. As we got closer, the bouncer got bigger and bigger. His arms were as big as my thighs on this former offensive lineman. He was a large Black man who ruined his football career by making bad choices in college. His tight black polo shirt with "Blew Bayou" in teal blue lettering fitting snug to the point that he should put on a 4XL and not a 3XL. But I'm not going to argue with him. If there is one thing I learned in my law enforcement career, if the man is that big, they don't need to know how to fight and don't let them get on top of you.

"What's up, brother? How's the talent tonight?" I asked in my gravely biker voice.

"IDs," was all he said.

"You got it." I reached into my back packet and retrieved my wallet on the chain and took out my fake driver's license.

Chris took his ID out of his canvas wallet by peeling the Velcro open. There's one thing a grown man should not have; actually, two things—one, a canvas wallet with Velcro and the other are tennis shoes with Velcro straps. That's just not right. He handed the big man his ID and stared at him in awe.

The bouncer handed our IDs back to us and said, "Five bucks."

I handed him a ten-dollar bill and asked, "Good?"

He nodded and pulled opened the door for us.

Ahhh, the sweet smell of cigarette smoke, stale beer, baby oil, hairspray, an array of perfumes and colognes, and mixtures of other not-so-pleasant fragrances. The thumping music was so loud that it started to hurt my head. The darkness of the bar was broken up with flickering red, blue, green, and yellow lights as well as a giant disco ball above the stage. A pool table in the back was occupied by two men playing for each other's paychecks while being cheered on by their buddies and a couple of dancers trying to gain their attention.

The bar was littered with local men riding out the time and drinking cheap liquor before meeting their demise with their wives at home, wishing their women looked and danced like the ones before them. The more they drink, the more they will. How does the saying go? No one is ugly at 2:00 a.m.

The stage is a half-circle with a brass pole in the center occupied by a bikini-wearing blonde woman. Whoops, now just the bottoms. That was quick. Her tattoos were tastefully done with her left arm from shoulder to elbow completely covered. The iconic stripper song, "Cherry Pie" by Warrant, begins to play on the loudspeakers. Now it's a party! I started to become mesmerized by the dancing and gyrating of the pretty exotic dancer and lose focus on why I'm here.

"Get me a beer." I ordered Chris as he rolled his eyes.

I moved to sniffer's row to get a better look. The young lady made eye contact with me as she swings around the pole like she has done a thousand times. There is only one other guy sitting in the soft maroon faux leather chairs. I sat down to take in all the sights and sounds of the place that used to be my second home. Not this bar, but one just like it.

I removed my Zippo lighter from the internal pocket of my vest along with the pack of Marlboro Lights. I placed a cigarette in between my lips with exaggeration and lighted it without taking my eyes off the pretty dancer. I felt that James Dean would have been proud of me at this point.

As "Diamond" crawled toward me, eyes piercing through me like a laser, I focused on her hair, her face, her arms, anything but her breasts. I'm working here, I'm not here for pleasure. Ah, hell, screw it! Wow, beautiful! She shimmied and shook toward me as I smiled and reached for a five-dollar bill to tuck into her bright red G-string.

"Thanks, baby," was all she said as she moved to the next sucker to help her pay for paralegal classes at the community college.

Chris snuck up behind me and handed me a bottle of Budweiser. I reached out for it and saw the multicolored glitter all over my hand from slapping "Diamond's" butt. Chris tapped me on the shoulder and nodded to the direction of the back room where the private dances take place.

"Joy is in there waiting for us."

"I'll follow."

This guy better not fuck me over is all I could think. I winked at "Diamond" before I turned and took a drag of my smoke, then followed Chris to the back of the bar. When we reached the back, another very large Black man was standing in front of the red crushed velvet curtains. Did she hire the Chicago Bears offensive line?

"Joy's waiting for you," in his best Barry White voice.

Chris walked past him, I nodded in acknowledgment.

"Joy! What's up, baby?" Chris said as he sauntered into the room like he was a pimp.

"Don't you baby me, you fat fuck! Where's my shit?"

Joy was still waiting for Chris to sell the rest of her kilos and get her the money. That is why I am here.

She sat at a round table with a dim light hanging above it. There was just enough light to see her shape and outline but not details. A drink with an umbrella and red straw in a clear glass sat on the table in front of her. She picked it up and swirled the ice cubes around before setting it down. The glass sweated onto the table with beads of water. She bypassed the straw and took a sip of her drink, then returned it to the ring on the table.

"Joy, this is Preacher, my cousin from Des Moines. He runs a motorcycle club and bought the rest of the 'crank.' But he needs more," Chris said, waiting for a response.

Joy looked me over, inspecting me and giving me the hairy eyeball. It made me a little uneasy to be honest. This little Asian woman can probably mess me up with a karate kick to the face. Maybe that's being stereotypical, but she is a fourth-degree black belt.

"What's yer name?" she questioned while stirring the drink.

"Preacher."

"Preacher, what?"

"Just Preacher."

"Just Preacher? Like Madonna or Prince?"

"Yep."

She thought about that for a few moments.

"Do you know whose territory this is? The Sons of Violence. Do you know who they are?" she asked with a thick Asian accent. I really had to concentrate on every word she said.

The music blaring in my head and trying to hear and understand Joy was one of the biggest cognitive issues I've ever had.

I nodded my head in response and told her I'm familiar with them.

"What club are you with?" she asked.

"Pale Rider's MC," I replied, standing a little taller.

"I don't know them."

"You will. Look, I got your money in a safe location. I wasn't bringing it to the club in the off chance of getting rolled. You want the money, you meet me, and I'll give it to you. But I need more product."

"Crank or Coke?" she asked.

I gambled. "Both."

She thought it over for a moment. I felt like I was being set up. But I always thought like that during an undercover operation. She got out her phone from her purse that was so small the phone was the only thing in it. She appeared to be texting someone. A minute later, she answered me.

"How much you want?"

"A key of each."

"Done. Meet me at my house in thirty minutes," she said as she handed me a piece of paper with an address on it.

I looked it over, folded it up, and put in the lower right exterior pocket of my vest. Chris said something to

Joy as we turned and walked out of her "office." We walked through the club, and I had to watch one more dance for the road to "help me focus." 'Diamond' was finishing her set, and the DJ was announcing the next dancer, "Gypsy." What song does she start her set with? "Girls, Girls, Girls" by Mötley Crüe, of course. I wonder how many girls I've seen dance to this song.

"Diamond" stepped off the stage and walked to me with our eyes locked. While holding her earnings and the clothes she shed, she leaned to me and gave me a kiss on the cheek. She handed me a piece of paper and smiled as she walked away, looking back to me before she opened the dressing room door. That is an ass I could bounce a quarter off.

As soon as we got to the truck, I called Adam and told him of the location change. We already knew where Joy lived due to the intel that we had gathered. I had forty thousand dollars stowed under the seat of my truck while we went into the strip club. Fortunately, Adam was watching the truck so no drunk broke in and took it. I really don't know how I would explain that to the county attorney. It was hard enough to get him to agree for us to use it as buy money and then get another forty thousand to buy the other kilos.

I pulled up alongside Adam as he handed me a small duffle bag with the buy money. Now I have eighty thousand dollars in cash in my truck with a guy who would easily try to roll me to take it. He would fail, but he would try.

I turned onto Joy's street and proceeded toward her house. Her BMW was parked in the driveway with no other vehicles on the street or in the driveways of the other houses. There were no working streetlights on the cul-de-sac. Again, this is by design. One light was visible in her house, what appeared to be a living room. A shadow moved across the room. I turned off the headlights as I parked behind her car. This way, if something happens and she tries to drive away, I have her blocked in.

"Are you fuckers setting me up?" I sternly asked Chris in hopes he was not going to lie to me.

"Na, man, I don't know what she has planned."

"Bullshit," I quietly said as I surveyed the area trying to find a signature of Murphy's law.

I turned the ignition off and waited. The engine made its final sputters and settled. I paused before opening the door. Something wasn't right, it's quiet, still, dark. When I was in the Marine Corps and we were on patrol in the jungles, we would come to an area that a possible ambush point would be. Danger close. The hairs on the back of my neck would raise up as little antennas, telling me not to move because something bad is about to happen. The raised hairs have now reappeared.

The door hinges creaked as I unlatched the door handle and slowly opened it. As I stepped out and stayed behind the opened door for cover, I glanced over at Chris. He was sitting in the seat while bent over tying his shoe, or appears to be tying his shoe.

Then I hear it...*pop, pop, pop, pop, pop!*

The impacts of the rounds striking the hood and windshield of my truck.

Another series...*pop, pop, pop, pop, pop!*

The rounds also impacting on the sheet metal of my truck. The sound of the gunfire disrupting the cool quiet night, tearing through the metal and glass with whizzes and pops passing me. The rhythmic trigger pull of the assailant affirmed the knowledge of the firearm.

Chris was still crouched over, trying to take cover and not be hit by a wayward shot aimed for me. He has something in his hand, but I was unable to verify what it was until I saw the blinding flash. I didn't hear anything, just the flash. An instant sharp pain in my abdomen brought me to my knees. I returned fire with my Glock into my truck. Three rounds impacting Chris on his left side and one to the left side of his head. The side window splattered with crimson liquid and brain matter seeping into the spiderweb cracks of the broken glass. Chris stayed slumped in that position with his final breath exhaling from his body in a gradual sigh.

My side hurt. Not like a stinging pain but like a side ache after running for six miles. I felt nauseated and weak. Still resting on my knee, I peered through the only piece of intact glass that I could find, trying to see where the shooter is.

Where is she? Listen…

God, my side burns!

The smell of gun powder and smoke stuck in the cab of the truck was making me lose focus. I knew Adam had heard the shots, where is he? I needed to get my rifle. I looked over my shoulder and tried to focus through the darkness of any glimmer of hope from the saving grace of my partner. Maybe he's flanking and sneaking in through the back. That's a good idea, great job, Adam!

Another series of shots rang out, hitting the concrete driveway and the grill of the truck. She has adjusted fire, trying to hit me from under the pickup.

Get to the back!

I crawled to the back of the truck as fast as I possibly could. It resembled the dream where I'm running as fast as I can and not gaining any ground. I reached the rear quarter panel by the wheel and noticed the trail of blood I left behind.

That's a lot of blood!

I felt a pain in my left knee like I twisted it. I reached down and felt a sticky substance. It was too dark to see, but I knew what it was, the bitch shot me! That would explain the amount of blood loss. I focused my failed vision test down the street looking for the calvary while listening for something or someone moving.

Why hasn't anyone called the cops?

I focused on my breathing and attempted to slow it down. One thing I learned when bleeding is the more your heart races, the faster blood loss you will incur.

Breathe!

I focused on the figure walking in the middle of the street. Only a shadow, no distinguishing features. I tried to concentrate through the pain and the haziness of my fading life.

Is that Adam?

No lights have come on, no sirens, no people screaming, no vehicles, and no dogs barking.

This is not good.

The figure gets closer and closer in an ominous pace. The figure raises a weapon toward me.

I called out, "Adam! Adam! Is that you?"

I raised my Glock to the center figure of the three that I saw. It's not that there were three people, but I saw three people.

Again, I yelled, "Adam! Is that you?"

"Adam's gone." The most piercing words I could ever hear.

I saw a bright light and a large boom as I felt a burning sensation on my right cheek and ear.

Fuck! He shot my ear!

I dropped my Glock in my lap as my right hand went to my ear, holding it in immense pain. Blood seeping through my fingers. Another flash and boom. The round made a flawless pencil-size circle through the rear quarter panel over my left shoulder. I regained my composure the best that I could and regained control of my blood soak, slippery pistol. I took aim with both eyes open and squinted.

I depressed the five-and-a-half-pound trigger pull and fired a wayward shot over the figure. I generated all my strength and power from within and steadied my right arm. My hand, sticky, adhering to the polymer grip of the Austrian handgun. Again, I fired. The recoil of the loosely held firearm startled me to regain consciousness. And then I let loose… *Boom, boom, boom, boom, boom!*

Each round hitting its mark. All five rounds impacting on center mass. The figure fell to his knees and then to his face. One arm outstretched to the side and the other underneath him. The clank of the rifle from falling to the concrete street echoed between the residences in the cul-de-sac. I applied pressure to the wound on my side and realized I have a hole in my favorite vest.

Gotdamit!

Multiple shots from close by struck the side of the pickup. I was able to tell that the shots came from my left. I looked under the truck and saw the unforgettable stiletto heel shoes of the lovely Asian stripper, Joy.

"Fuck her!" I said out loud to myself, or maybe it was loud enough for others to hear.

I propped myself up with the muzzle of my Glock, not a practice I would instruct. Once I got to my knee, I assisted myself further by utilizing the rear bumper as support. I stood up and pointed my Glock Model 23 at Joy and pulled the trigger. The muzzle flash blinded me from watching the hot spinning steel crash through the cranial cavity of the charming exotic dancer. Her lifeless body crumpled to the wet grass with a thud.

I assessed the area for more weapon-wielding drug dealers. Nothing. I made my way to Joy by limping and cringing in pain. As I stood over her body, I tapped her leg for a reaction. Nothing. My Glock's slide was locked in the rear position, indicating an empty chamber. I ejected the spent magazine with my thumb, then reached into my back pocket for a full mag and inserted it. With two thumbs, I pushed down on the lever and released the slide catch with a solid metal clank. The sound echoed in my head.

The sounds of the sirens slowly got closer. I could not see the red and blue emergency lights yet, but knew they were on their way. I stumbled to the edge of the front yard and fell along the landscaping around the mailbox and the curb. Still with my Glock in my hand, I felt my fading breath become more and more labored. A police squad car came to a screeching stop in front of me with the flashing headlights and overhead red and blues illuminating me. I looked up enough for him or her to know I'm still alive and then I heard…

"Over here, over here!" The officer waving frantically toward the mouth of the cul-de-sac.

The officer approached me with gun in hand and put his non-firing hand on my back. "Are you hit, where are you hit?"

All I said was, "Is Adam okay?"

CHAPTER 28

My vision went from foggy to red to black. I woke up in a hospital five days later from a medical-induced coma to restore the blood loss. When I woke up, I was in an empty hospital room. I tried to regain focus and an understanding what had happened and where I was. I felt a foreign object in my left hand. I held it up and realized it was an emergency button for a nurse to render aid. I pushed the button with my thumb three times as if it were the trigger mechanism for a claymore.

A young female nurse with blonde hair stepped in through the light fabric curtain.

"Good, you're awake," she said calmly, like she was waiting for me to wake from an afternoon nap on a beach.

"My name is Lisa. I'm your PA for the afternoon. Your family just left and will be back in a couple of hours. Do you know where you are?"

My throat sore from the tube they removed, I tried to clear my head and remove the fogginess of the painkillers and antibiotics pumped through my body for the last five days.

"The hospital?"

"Yes, you are at Mercy in Des Moines. You were life-flighted here. We didn't think you were going to make it. You lost a lot of blood. How do you feel?"

"Where's Adam? I need to see Adam."

"Oh, sweetie. Let me get the doctor."

I grabbed ahold of her wrist and held on with all the power that I could muster and asked again.

"Where is Adam?"

She reached out for my hand and held it while it clasped on to her wrist and simply shook her head. Lisa bent down and gave me a hug the best that she could without putting her arms around me and whispered, "I'm so sorry."

I later found out that Adam was found in the driver's seat of the Tahoe two blocks away from the shootout. He was slumped over the steering wheel with a single shot through the left side of his head. He was killed instantly without pain or knowledge of his assassin. His gun was in his left hand and his phone in his right. The Motorola flip phone was open and the beginning of a text the read: "On my w…"

CHAPTER 29

The next year, I testified in federal court against Mikey, Jeremy, James, and Sgt. First-Class Raburn. The day of court, I trimmed my goatee to a respectable length, removed my earring, bracelets, rings, and necklace. I placed all the jewelry in a wooden box and set it in my gun safe along with my wallet with my undercover contents. I held up my biker colors and put my trigger finger through the bullet hole where Chris shot me, reminiscing about that night I lost a brother. I folded the vest nicely and set it on the top shelf of the safe.

When I shut the safe, I felt that I locked the past and false persona away for good. It almost felt like I lost a piece of me and took my edge away. My heart was heavy for the loss of Adam. For the loss of the unknown deputy sheriff. For the work I, we, had put in and now it's over.

I had a lot of time to think about all the drug deals and contraband we removed from the streets while driving to Sioux City for court. It was about an hour-and-a-half drive to the courthouse. When I arrived, I met with Russ, Brandon, Jason, and Nick along with the federal prosecutor. We had a brief meeting in a secure room until it was time to enter the court room.

I stayed behind until it was time for me to enter the federal courtroom. When a US Marshal came to get me, the uneasiness of the stress and nerves of the magnitude of this case overtook me. I stood up and had to catch my breath as I held on to the table for balance. The Marshal stepped to me and placed his hand on my shoulder for comfort.

"You did a fantastic thing here, Officer. We are all very proud of what you and your team did. Now let's go finish these fuckers off."

I looked up at him and gave a nervous but calming smile.

As I stood outside the courtroom waiting for my name to be called, I heard the prosecutor call his next witness, Officer Phil Quick.

FINAL PAGE

Tears of a Cop

I have been where you fear to go
I have seen what you fear to see
I have done what you fear to do
All these things I have done for you

I am the one you lean upon
The one you cast your scorn upon
The one you bring your troubles to
All these people I've been for you

The one you ask to stand apart
The one you feel should have no heart
The one you call the man in blue
But I am human just like you

And through the years I've come to see
That I'm not what you ask of me
So take this badge and take this gun
Will you take it? Will anyone

And when you watch a person die
And hear a battered baby cry
Do you think that you can be
All those things you ask of me?

ABOUT THE AUTHOR

The author, Phil Queen, is a former US Marine and a retired police officer in Iowa after twenty years. During that time, he was a narcotics investigator and was assigned to other law enforcement agencies in Iowa as an undercover operative. He is currently working on his BS degree and enjoys spending quality time with his family during his retirement. This book started out to help mitigate stress and PTS, which has evolved into a love for writing. This is the first book of many to come.

CPSIA information can be obtained
at www.ICGtesting.com
Printed in the USA
LVHW111438200321
681997LV00024B/423/J